FOR CARLENE Y
CHARMING A. D
TO HAVE MET

Emerald

Safe

a collection of erotic stories

◦‿◦

Emerald

◦‿◦

1001 Nights Press

HMK 2015

Safe: a collection of erotic stories
Copyright © 2014 Emily McCay, writing as Emerald
Published by 1001 Nights Press
Edited by Sharazade
Cover design by CoverDomme

ISBN-13: 978-0692307045
ISBN-10: 0692307044

All rights reserved. No part of this publication may be reproduced, stored in or introduced into a retrieval system, or transmitted, in any form, or by any means (electronic, mechanical, photocopying, recording, or otherwise) without the prior written permission of the copyright owner.

The scanning, uploading, and distribution of this book via the Internet or via any other means without the permission of the publisher is illegal and punishable by law.

This is a work of fiction. Names, characters, places, brands, media, and incidents are either the product of the author's imagination or are used fictitiously.

Table of Contents

Power over Power

I pulled open the glass door against the glaring Saturday morning sun. The heavily windowed walls offered little relief from its brightness as I blinked and looked around the lobby. Dominic sat at his desk across from the front counter.

One month before, I had watched Dominic on the first night of class as he stood at the front of the studio and introduced the defense system in which he would be training us. The students stood in a row in front of him, dressed the same way he was in sneakers, black t-shirts with the royal blue Krav Maga logo on the chest, and loose, lightweight black pants with matching royal blue stripes down the sides.

"Krav Maga is not like traditional martial arts," he had explained. "Traditional martial arts involve sparring, a back-and-forth, a focus on skill. Krav Maga is about dropping somebody – knocking someone out within ten seconds so you can get away." He met the eyes of each student in the line in front of him. "It's also not about size. The point of Krav is that it puts everyone on an equal playing field, focusing on universal vulnerabilities that anyone can exploit, regardless of size."

His voice was calm, assured, serious. I had watched him, captivated. Dominic didn't necessarily look like a self-defense expert. He was only slightly taller than I was, probably five-foot-ten. His build was slim and athletic. The denseness of his muscles, however, had been evident in the resounding thuds that reverberated off the studio walls as he demonstrated kicks, punches, knees, and elbows on the punching bag at the front of the room as the students watched in silence.

Despite the subject matter, there was no bravado or machismo in his countenance. I had seen from the pictures and accompanying labels hanging in the lobby that Dominic taught traditional martial arts as well as Krav Maga. While I had never taken any myself, I sensed in him the understated confidence I had observed before in martial artists – an exquisite self-possession and understanding of their capabilities, the assurance such that there was no need to prove anything to anyone. It was like they had power over their own power. It served them rather than the other way around. There was no compulsion to use it, to put it on display; it was just there, second nature, if it was ever needed.

Dominic looked up at my entrance.

"Hi, Jackie."

I smiled at him and glanced at the clock. Saturday-morning class was optional, a makeup class for those who missed any of the three sessions held during the week or who just wanted an extra review. I was about five minutes early, but there didn't seem to be anyone else around.

He followed my gaze. "You're the only one here so far. People often trickle in around starting time on Saturdays. You can have a seat if you want, or go on in and start warming up."

I sat on the bench perpendicular to his desk, and he smiled and turned back to his computer. I didn't need to look at Dominic to feel the way he was affecting me. It happened just from being in the same room with him. It was something that went beyond looks, beyond personality, beyond simple attraction. It was pure heat, like a raw power of undiluted wanting, craving, hunger. I felt it when I watched the nonchalance with which he taught the methodology used by the Israeli army for hand-to-hand combat – a methodology designed, ultimately, to kill people. I watched the skill, control, focus of the lightning flashes of movement, heard the cracking thuds against padding that seemed effortless to him, and felt the raw heat in my core. Every movement he executed was exactly what was called for; nothing more, nothing less. Power was cultivated in him so deeply it simply came forth whenever it served.

And I wanted to fuck him so badly I could hardly stand still.

As I sat there now, he glanced at the clock again. "Hmm. Maybe people had a little too much partying on a Friday night." He chuckled as he stood up. "I've never had attendance this low on a Saturday."

"Yeah, I imagine you want to cancel," I babbled, standing nervously.

Dominic shrugged. "It's up to you. You can certainly take off if you'd like. If you want to stay, I'll work you."

A shiver went through me, and I tried not to shudder visibly. I glanced around, not sure if I did want to take the studio with Dominic by myself. I knew his focus was strictly professional, and I might end up making a fool of myself as I practically drooled over him.

"Uh, okay. If you don't mind," I responded, my mouth appearing to ignore all the considerations that had just run through my mind.

"No, come on in." He indicated the studio with a jerk of his head and led me into it. I moved to the far end toward the supply room and set my bag and purse down on the bench.

As we began stretching, my breath quickened. The training hadn't even begun, and already I knew this was a mistake. I wasn't going to be able to handle this kind of undivided attention from Dominic. Even if he were interested in what I was, which I had no reason to believe he was, the studio's walls were made of glass, making the view from the street wide open. He wasn't about to fuck me with that kind of visibility.

I had to get out of there.

"Okay, you remember the way we learned early in the week to defend against a choke hold?" Dominic asked.

"Yeah," I answered, clearing my throat. Dominic approached me, and I almost backed up, not trusting myself if he touched me.

"Show me what you remember." He reached forward and placed both hands around my neck, facing me. My breath caught, and I snapped my hands up and slammed my forearms into his, breaking the grip.

"Good," he said, stepping back. "Let's try it up against the wall."

I was painfully aware of my ragged breathing and the wetness between my legs as Dominic leaned into me, wrapping his hands around my neck and pushing me back against the wall. I defended again and had to consciously resist pressing my hand between my legs.

"Okay, grab a kick shield," Dominic said, nodding at a stack in the corner. "I'm going to demonstrate the kick we learned on Wednesday. Remember, start with your weight on the kicking foot – hop quickly to the other foot and kick while you're in the air. The momentum increases your power. Then recoil immediately. Always recoil right away. Limbs not up against you are vulnerable to being grabbed."

I nodded, trying to focus. Dominic backed up, and I crouched in position with the kick pad in front of me. Dominic's foot snapped forward, and I was almost knocked backward by the force of the impact even as the padding absorbed most of it. I shuddered as I imagined what such a blow would be like without the shield.

"Your turn," Dominic took the pad from me.

I did my best to kick the sexual frustration out of me as I slammed first my right then my left foot into the kick pad with a grunt. I alternated back and forth until Dominic told me to stop.

The elevated heart rate and adrenaline pumping through me had not served the desired purpose at all.

"Do you remember the series we learned earlier in the week?" Dominic demonstrated in the air the series of punches, kicks, and elbow slams to get out of a headlock and render the assailant on the ground. I nodded.

"Okay, let's try it." Dominic fitted his arm around my neck from behind and held firmly. My breath caught, and

I almost pressed back against him. I caught myself and mimed the series, stopping each move just short of actual impact with him. My breath was ragged again when I finished. The tingling in my pussy was to the point of distraction.

"Are you okay?" Dominic asked.

"Yeah," I squeaked out, almost wincing at the hoarseness of my voice. I cleared my throat. "Fine. Go right ahead," I said, managing to sound almost normal.

He turned me around and grabbed me around the neck again, and immediately I couldn't breathe – and it wasn't because his hold was too strong. I started the series, slamming my elbow back toward his chest, halting right before it made contact with him. Suddenly I forgot the next move and stopped.

"Don't stop," Dominic said. "Don't ever stop, Jackie."

"I forgot the next move," I stared to explain as Dominic turned me around.

"I know you did. But you're training yourself all the time here, and you don't ever want to train yourself to pause or freeze. If you forget what you're doing" – his eyes were serious as they penetrated mine – "just start throwing punches."

I held his gaze and managed to nod.

He backed up. "You want to grab some water?"

I nodded again and walked over to my bag as he moved to the side of the room to put the kick shield back. I took a drink, facing the bench, and set my water bottle down.

Suddenly a body was up against me from behind, arm rough around my neck. I was in a headlock. It took me just a second to realize I needed to defend myself, and I snapped an elbow back and tried to whirl, realizing it was too late.

Dominic whipped me around and pressed me against the wall. "Okay, you weren't expecting me there. You weren't ready, and you paused. Assailants don't wait until you're ready. You have to be prepared all the time." He eased his hold on me and backed up. I was breathless, staring in his eyes as my pussy tingled insistently.

"I'm going to grab some gloves," he said, moving to the supply room a few feet away.

He opened the door and disappeared through it as I stared at it. I swallowed. As if drawn by a magnet, my feet began to step toward the supply room. The door was open, and I could hear Dominic rummaging around inside as I approached. I reached the door and silently stepped through it.

Dominic's back was to me. He pulled a pair of gloves from the top of a pile and turned, stopping when he saw me.

I was already in the room, where I wasn't supposed to be. There was no way to back out gracefully now. For a few seconds there was silence.

"I want you to–" my voice, already tiny and faltering, failed me after those four words.

Dominic took a step forward, his expression questioning. He raised his eyebrows and cocked an ear toward me. "You want what?"

My breathing was uneven; I felt like I did when I was already close to orgasm. The intensity wasn't lending itself to articulation. I moved forward as well.

"I want," my voice halted again, but this time only for a split second. "I want you to fuck me."

I whispered it, knowing I was barely audible, and looked down at the ground, my cheeks flaming. I felt

Dominic's eyes on me and told myself the worst he could do was say no, and I could turn around and leave and never come back. The all-encompassing fixation of wanting him overruled humiliation in me as the room stayed silent for a few seconds.

Dominic's motions were deliberate as he moved toward and then past me. My eyes widened. I didn't move.

The quiet, solid thud of the door closing sent a jolt of heat through me that almost made me dizzy. I barely breathed as I started to turn around.

But he was already back in front of me. Dominic moved in so that he was almost touching me, close enough that I felt weak but not actually making contact. He looked down at me.

"You want me to fuck you," he repeated. His tone was neutral.

I trembled, wanting to touch him but feeling frozen. Still looking at the ground, I nodded.

With characteristic efficiency of motion, he reached with one finger and pulled my chin up. A shudder ran through me as I felt his power – the power I saw in every move he made, that he exuded at the front of the class, that he spoke when he told us what we were capable of, that coiled and expelled from him whenever he slammed any part of his body into the punching bag. The power that lived unquestioned within him, so seamlessly that it was as though it wouldn't exist without him.

I moved my eyes to his. Dominic pushed forward and kissed me, hard, his body pressing against mine as I hit the wall behind me. I thrashed against him, my hands ripping at his t-shirt as I fought to breathe. I felt like I could already come.

Dominic placed one hand behind my neck and gripped my waist, pulling my body even closer to his. I pulled at his shirt again and he let go of me and stripped it off, reaching to pull mine off as well before returning his hands to the solid grip of my body and his mouth to an unrelenting kiss. I could feel his erection against me as he slowed down and eased back.

"We'd need a condom," he whispered, looking down at me.

My eyes felt out of focus as I looked back at him. "I have them in my purse," I whispered back, barely recognizing my own voice.

Dominic stepped back, and I walked shakily to the door in my pants, sneakers, and sports bra. I opened it and stepped through, blinking at the sunlight streaming in through the glass walls. It felt like a different world.

I retrieved my purse and reentered the supply room unsteadily. As I stepped through the door Dominic's hard chest hit me from behind, his arm instantaneously around my neck. I drew a quick breath and rammed my elbow to within an inch of his chest, my own chest heaving.

He whirled me around and pushed me back up against the wall.

"Good reaction time that time," he said, his voice low. "Particularly under the circumstances." I felt the hardness of his cock pressing against my hip. Slowly he brought one hand up to grip my throat, then the other to join it.

"You know what to do now?" His voice was a whisper. The question wasn't really a question. We had just practiced it in the studio.

I nodded. He looked at me, not moving.

"I don't want to," I whispered. I heard the tremble in my voice.

Dominic nodded slowly, eyes still on mine. He could have held me in place with them alone. He moved one hand to stoke a finger along my jawline, his eyes following it. His other hand stayed in place at my throat. He licked his lips and looked back at me.

Suddenly his grip tightened as he lifted me up against the wall by my neck. My jaw dropped, my feet hanging loosely without the ground beneath them. I was at exactly eye level with Dominic now, his hand against the sides of my neck in a way that somehow barely hurt.

My pussy started to drip.

Dominic's eyes blazed into mine as he reached and ran a finger from my collarbone down to the top of my sports bra. Slowly he lowered me back to the ground and pushed my sports bra up, grabbing my breasts with a firmness just short of painful. My breath came to a fiery halt in my throat.

"Breathe," he whispered, looking in my eyes. It was an order he often gave during class. I obeyed, expelling the breath caught in my throat and deliberately guiding in another one.

Dominic reached up and removed my ponytail holder, then lifted my sports bra over my head and pulled me forward. He guided me across the room to a stack of floor mats about waist-high. Pressing me up against them, he ran his hand up the back of my neck and grabbed my hair near my scalp. As he kissed me I whimpered, involuntarily gyrating against him. He lowered his hands and yanked my pants and panties down to my knees, lifting me to the stack of mats and pulling them the rest of the way off almost before I realized what was happening. I kicked my sneakers off and looked at him, breathing heavily.

Dominic lifted me back to the ground and turned me around, one hand holding my hip, the other tracing lightly over the front of my body. His fingers strayed casually, rising over the swell of one breast, dragging lightly across the nipple, then drifting down the other side and on to the next one. The reminder to breathe was gone. I felt like I had forgotten how.

I wanted him to throw me down, ram his cock into me and fuck me hard, take full control of me, of him, of – everything. I tried to wiggle impatiently and realized that despite the calmness of his movements, the grip he had on me was like a clothespin on tissue paper. I felt his breath on my ear, steady in comparison to my almost frantic panting. Slowly he moved his hand from my breasts to the back of my neck again, sliding it up through my hair and gripping into a fist. I caught my breath.

"Well, conveniently enough, I want to fuck you too, Jackie," he whispered smoothly, and my legs trembled. "And I think I know what you want me to do. You want me to hold you down, fuck you hard, get pretty rough with you." I wondered if, for the first time, I would come without actually being touched. "You're looking for power. In your own way, getting fucked rough like that will make you feel powerful. Is that right?" My vision was becoming fuzzy, and I could hardly make sense of the words he was saying.

Dominic let go of my hip and slid his hand across my stomach, up over my breasts and finally to my throat.

"Everything you're looking for, Jackie, you already have inside you." The tone of his whisper had changed, and I barely had time to process the words before he whipped me around, shoving my mouth open lightly with his teeth as he kissed me again. He held my hair in a fist of steel and moved his other hand back to my body, lightly brushing my ribcage. He pulled back and watched the slow movement of his fingers, gliding like molasses over my skin.

I whimpered desperately. He hadn't even touched my pussy, and I felt close to a kind of climax of which I didn't know the meaning. It felt like a near euphoria combined with a vague but deep fear that together seemed to be pushing tears toward the surface.

"Dominic," I pleaded. My voice trembled like a blade of grass in the breeze. He looked up at me.

I realized then what he was doing. He was making me wait, making me feel, making me experience every single nuance, every detail, every thing that was in me, in my body, instead of slamming it all away.

And suddenly I wondered if that was what having power over power meant.

The tears flowed out of me like an orgasm, fully beyond my control, my breath turning to a silent sob that felt somehow calm, even peaceful, as I felt a space open up in me I wasn't sure I had ever felt before. Dominic's eyes stayed on mine.

The wave moved through me, and Dominic dropped his finger to my clit. I gasped and climaxed as soon as he moved it, orgasm bursting forth in a rush so overpowering I almost felt I would lose consciousness. Steady, unabated screams pulsed through me as Dominic held my gaze as well as my balance with his unyielding grip at my neck. When it was done I fell limp, my entire body slick with sweat, legs shaking and hanging like string over the stack of mats as Dominic lifted me to sit on top of them.

He lowered me onto my back and let go of my hair, then backed up and retrieved my purse. Hands shaking, I reached and fumbled through it in my horizontal position until I found the little zippered pouch. Extracting a condom from it, I pushed it into his hand.

I heard my purse drop to the floor and the package rip open as Dominic backed up. He slid me up further on the stack of mats and leapt lightly onto them himself, pushing between my legs. My eyes were closed, and I opened them as he hovered above me. I was far beyond words, knowing only what was in my body.

"Breathe," Dominic whispered again as he dropped his body onto mine, plunging into me and grasping my shoulders as his breath rushed against my ear. He thrust into me with rhythmic strength as I lay like a doll, sprawled powerlessly across the hard foam beneath me. Dominic pumped hard, holding my hips solidly. His breathing changed as he thrust just a bit harder and came inside me, my body like a deflated balloon, a beautiful, motionless receptacle for his come.

I closed my eyes again as he finished, feeling a sorrow at the impending loss of contact with his body. When he pulled out, I opened my eyes and turned to him. He leapt off the stack of mats and reached to help me down. I stopped at the edge, not ready to stand up yet.

In a daze I looked at the floor, my body shaking. Dominic's low voice broke the silence.

"Whatever is in you, whatever you're feeling – feel it. Don't hide from it. Don't try to 'beat' it. Be with it until you understand it, until you know where it comes from." I frowned at the floor. "Then it won't rule you anymore."

I raised my eyes to his as he finished the sentence. Sweat dripped from the side of my forehead down to my neck as my quick breaths punctuated the silence in the room.

"That's what power is," Dominic said. "It doesn't have anything to do with force or subjugation."

I looked down at his hand as he held it out to me again and allowed my body to slide off the mats. My feet on the floor felt foreign.

I gathered my clothes and dressed slowly. Dominic handed me my purse as I straightened, and we walked together to the door. I turned to him; without a word he grabbed the back of my neck and kissed me, rendering me immediately breathless as I braced myself against the door with one hand.

He let go of me slowly. My fingers slipped from the door as he took a step back.

"See you Monday." Dominic's hand brushed the small of my back once before he stepped forward and turned the knob.

Hers to Keep

"Ten! Nine! Eight! Seven!..."

It was the pause between each shout, the literal split second of anticipation before the next number, where Leslie felt like she was. Perpetually in that place of waiting, watching, wondering, the in-between of what was happening rather than actually living among it.

Of course, that was a bit of an exaggeration. The countdown to the annual climax mere seconds away just seemed to highlight the anticlimactic feeling of her current circumstances. Between jobs, between relationships, between any experience that seemed exciting or interesting in her life.

She watched the glittery ball on the oversized flat-screen TV as the frenzy around her grew until the shout of *"One – Happy New Year!"* reverberated in her ears and the ball dropped amid a flurry of camaraderie and confetti and chaos. The crowd in the room turned to the floor-to-ceiling windows to watch the barrage of fireworks that shattered the frigid air amidst the pandemonium of kissing, drinking, and laughing that took over the large suite for the next several minutes.

Leslie watched the colored sparks reflect in the window. Since the fireworks were shot from the park right across the street from the hotel, their view was unparalleled – one of the reasons they'd chosen this hotel for their party. The presidential suite wasn't cheap, to be sure, but with 12 of them pitching in for the multi-hosted party, it had been doable. As Leslie turned back to watch the merriment around her and join in to a somewhat subdued degree, she conceded that the plan had been successful. More than 50 people filled the spacious suite in paper tiaras, hats, and banners that read "Happy New Year!" in glittering letters, and they all appeared to be having a good time.

And she was too, she acknowledged as she took a sip from her champagne flute. She was glad her friends had suggested the suite rental, citing the view of the fireworks, central location, and lack of next-day cleanup duties as justification for the financial splurge. Particularly right now, Leslie had noticed, hotels appealed to her – the lack of commitment, responsibility, ownership. Just a space of indulgence, catering to a specified period of carefree luxury. The perfect setting for a party, and for her, the start of a new year.

She suddenly noticed that her eyes had landed on the man she'd seen enter the room only about 10 minutes before midnight. She'd taken note of him then, no doubt, but she had no idea who he was or whom he knew there and felt no desire to approach him on her own.

Actually, that wasn't true. The desire was there. She squirmed uncomfortably, taking another drink of champagne. Sometimes her own shyness frustrated her. It was more that she didn't feel *comfortable* going up to him, especially since she was obviously not the only one who had noticed the particular presence he possessed, as he was now surrounded by a group of partygoers and appeared perfectly comfortable as the center of attention.

She stepped into the mob and made the rounds, placing chaste kisses on the cheeks of her closest friends and, with a bit of a blush, some of the new people she was just meeting tonight.

Without really trying, she eventually she found herself in the group surrounding the mysterious – albeit popular – stranger, and as her friend Ed kissed her cheek and turned to introduce him to her, she blushed harder.

"Leslie, this is Grant. He heads up the IT department at our branch in Colorado. Grant, this is Leslie, a good friend of mine."

"Pleasure to meet you," Grant said, his eyes on hers as he offered a warm handshake. Leslie nodded and returned the sentiment even as his touch made her body tingle. He was even more magnetizing up close than he'd appeared from across the room, his smile glittering like the ball that had just dropped in Times Square. She was suddenly sorry that the kissing part of the evening had just passed. She thought wistfully for a moment about her less shy friends and what they might do in this situation before she looked down, flustered, and let go of his hand.

She shifted to face the rest of the group, standing somewhat awkwardly between Grant and Ed as the conversation picked up where it had presumably left off. She could feel the heat of Grant's body next to her, and it made breathing more difficult.

"So where's Alicia?" Ed asked, and Grant nodded acknowledgment of the question as he took a drink.

"She skipped this trip, not wanting to be stuck watching me work on New Year's Eve," he laughed. "We didn't know about your party at the time."

He was married. Leslie dropped her eyes to his left hand, which she'd forgotten to check. She stared dully at the silver band there. A lightness in her that she hadn't even fully noticed yet plummeted, disappearing into the ether as Ed gave some response.

With a subtle sigh, Leslie excused herself a few moments later and returned to the bar in the corner of the suite's main room. Abandoning her champagne flute, she grabbed the ice scoop and a glass and looked around for the bottle of Scotch.

Leaning against the bar, she took a sip and looked out the window at the black sky, void now of its pyrotechnic display and filled again with only the still, chilly-looking glow of orange streetlights and a cloud-shrouded moon. A few of her co-hosts came over, and she swallowed her frustration and made an effort to join the conversation.

"Do you know where you want to sleep tonight, Leslie?" her friend Kayla asked. There were two bedrooms included on either side of the suite. While many would probably crash on the floor of the main room, it was understood that the party hosts were privy to the bedroom accommodations.

Leslie pointed to one of the doors. "I put my stuff in that one. I brought a sleeping bag and don't really mind sleeping on the floor if need be."

Kayla nodded and started to say something, then stopped and smiled over Leslie's shoulder.

Leslie turned and found Grant behind her holding the bottle of Scotch. He smiled at her, and she smiled back somewhat stiffly, doing her best to quell the attraction in her now that she knew he was married. He gestured toward her glass with the bottle, and she held it out to him with a shrug.

"I understand you're one of the hosts of this shindig. Great party," he said, raising his glass to her. "I'd suspected I'd be spending New Year's alone on a computer somewhere."

She nodded acknowledgment and couldn't help smiling.

"I knew Ed lived here and had gotten in touch with him about getting together later in the week, and he told me about this party," he continued. "As it turned out, I wrapped up what I needed to just in time to come ring in the new year. I'm glad, since it turns out I'll be flying back home tomorrow. Holiday or not, information systems don't take breaks." He smiled and took another drink.

"Well, your wife will probably be glad to see you," Leslie said lightly, reminding him that she knew he had one.

"Yes, she probably would have come with me if she'd known I'd be going to a party," he responded, showing no sign of embarrassment or hesitance at the mention of his wife. He met her eyes. "It's too bad. I'm sure she would have loved to meet you too." He trained that smile on her, and it seemed to emanate heat straight to her core. Leslie looked away and fumbled with her glass, finding the comment odd even as she tried fervently to ignore the tingling arousal Grant's attention set off throughout her body.

"We're in an open relationship," he continued easily as he lifted his glass to his lips.

"An open relationship," Leslie repeated. She tried not to display her ignorance. She'd heard the phrase, but she'd never personally known anyone who was in one.

"We have sex with other people," he clarified.

Leslie stared at him.

"Not that I mean to be implying anything." Grant's demeanor suddenly shifted to slight embarrassment, and Leslie realized her response was probably making him think she wasn't interested in such a thing regardless of what kind of relationship he and his wife had. The heat returned to her cheeks and, flustered, she realized she needed to say something.

"Do you mean – your wife knows you do that?" She blushed harder for having answered with something she immediately deemed one of the dumbest-sounding things she had said in some time. The truth was that at the words "other people," her breath had caught, and the dizzying effect he seemed to be having on her had increased exponentially. Was he hitting on her?

"It's not really something either of us 'does' that the other needs to 'know' about," he said, the smile back on his face. All discomfort had evaporated from his countenance, returning him to the self-assured state she was already finding familiar in him. "It's just the style of relationship we have. But in answer to your question, yes, we communicate openly about what we're up to."

Her next thought, of course, was that there was little to no privacy in this party setting – as large as the suite was, every room was filled with celebrating bodies, and not in the way he probably had in mind. He was leaving in the morning, eliminating the opportunity almost as soon as it had materialized. Despite her hesitance and confusion, the stab of disappointment this realization elicited almost physically hurt.

Grant's eyes were still on her. "I have a room here," he said quietly, as if reading her mind.

She looked up and met his eyes. For the second time his words blew open a door she had perceived as firmly shut. As she felt herself inhale, her breasts rising subtly as though yearning of their own accord to get closer to him, she realized she might get what she finally acknowledged a part of her had wanted since the moment she'd caught sight of this man walking through the door half an hour ago.

Let's get to it, that part of her said internally. She blinked at its forwardness; she wouldn't dream of saying the words out loud. That wasn't how she had sex. Whether or not she had felt inclined to, a part of her had always held such tendencies in check, insisting on knowing the various ins and outs of a situation, what she was seeking with the person in question, and whether it was likely to happen going in.

Admittedly, sometimes she spent so much time analyzing, scrutinizing, anticipating, the opportunity vanished right before her. But she preferred to have all her bases covered where sex was concerned, fretting about what she should do before and afterward, how she should act, whether she liked this person enough want more than sex, and vice versa. Sex as something spontaneous or even pleasure-focused didn't really exist in her world.

Thus, she blinked as the insistent internal voice – one she had almost never heard, or at least heeded – continued its song, seemingly assured of her acquiescence. Even as she mentally she shook her head, she found herself stepping forward, holding Grant's gaze, and giving an almost-nod as she took his arm. Calmly, solidly, he led her through the barrage of partygoers, all of whom appeared oblivious as he opened the door to the hallway and ushered her through it.

They walked in silence to the elevator. Leslie was nervous, and she was sure he knew it. Not only did she not usually have sex with people she'd just met, she had never done so at all with anyone who was spoken for. In fact, as she followed Grant through the door of his hotel room, a wave of panic washed over her. She stopped short.

"Are you sure your wife knows about this? Or, I mean, would be okay with it?"

Grant smiled at her as he let the door close behind her. "Let me just text her right now," he said, and Leslie felt instantly more at ease. It was clear he understood her concern. Nothing about how he acted seemed sneaky, underhanded, or lecherous, admittedly. Still, she remained silent as he turned his attention to the phone in his hand. She found herself staring at his strong, nimble fingers as they brushed over the tiny screen. She bit her lip.

"I don't know what she's doing tonight, so I don't know how quickly she'll get back to me, but she is aware of the situation now – or will be when she reads that," he said, setting the phone on the dresser. "And if I thought she wouldn't be okay with this, I wouldn't be doing it."

His easy manner disarmed her even as she still felt a bit unnerved. She jumped as the phone buzzed against the wood of the dresser. They both turned to it, and Grant picked it up.

He chuckled as he read the message. Then he turned it around for her to see.

"Hope I get to meet her sometime. Have fun!" it read simply, followed by a wink emoticon. Leslie's eyes moved to the top of the screen, where the message was attributed to "Alicia" in bold letters.

She blinked. Before she could do anything more, Grant stepped closer to her, his body almost touching her even as it seemed to still allow her an undefined space. Leslie's breath caught; after a beat, she looked up at him.

His kiss was softer than she expected, not the slightest bit rushed or aggressive. The unhurriedness seemed to spread through the rest of her body as their lips stayed together, his tongue swirling against hers in a way that somehow offered but didn't intrude, received but didn't push. As though it were meeting her exactly where she was.

She felt his hands at the zipper on the back of her dress, and as he pulled it down, she got wet. His actions were as seamless as his kiss as he let her dress drop, slid her panties down her legs, and stood back up to kiss her again, his arm wrapping around her waist and pulling her closer with the slightest increase in urgency. She stepped toward him, pressing her naked body against his fully clothed one as his hand slid down her hip.

He slipped a single finger into her waiting wetness. She gasped, astonished by the arousal the action elicited. In his unhurried fashion, he stroked inside her languidly, the intimacy of the connection making her feel physically weak.

As if he sensed this, Grant picked her up and carried her the few feet to the bed where he laid her gently down, her head landing on one of the plush pillows. He stepped back and started to loosen his tie, pausing once as he looked at her, his eyes sweeping over her body in the dim light from the streetlights below. Her breathing grew deeper under his gaze.

Resuming his actions, he pulled off his tie and continued undressing, his movements more efficient, though still not rushed. He extracted something from the pocket of his trousers before he dropped them on the floor and climbed onto the bed.

His hand returned between her legs, but rather than entering her, he began to stroke a finger slowly over her clit, which was slick with her arousal. Leslie gasped and gave a tiny whimper. Grant increased the pace and the pressure, and her body tingled as she squirmed under his touch.

"I've been wanting to watch you come since I first caught sight of you when I walked in tonight," he whispered against her ear, and the words prophesied their own request as Leslie's body convulsed, her back arching and limbs thrashing as tiny squeals emitted from her throat.

Grant slid the condom on then, and she spread her legs and welcomed him as he climbed on top of her. For the first time his actions were urgent, and he fucked her hard and solidly as she writhed and panted, wanting to pull him ever deeper as he grunted above her. He groaned in her ear as he came, pushing into her while she gripped his flesh and squeezed herself around him until they both fell, exhausted, against each other and the white hotel sheets beneath them.

Grant answered Kayla's earlier question about where Leslie would sleep by pulling her to his side, settling himself behind her, and pulling the covers up over them. Leslie let out a breath, allowing sleep to sneak up on her as she relaxed against his body in the warm hotel bed.

Leslie woke to the rustling of a suitcase being unzipped, her eyes blinking open to the first sunlight of the new year as it seeped through the sheer curtains.

"I'm sorry – I was trying not to wake you," Grant said pleasantly as he folded a shirt and placed it in the suitcase now open beside her on the bed.

"No problem," she said a bit shyly, glancing around for her dress as she held the covers against her.

"I hung your dress in the bathroom." Grant nodded at the doorway as he nestled a belt into the suitcase beside the shirt. He moved away to face the closet, taking his time removing a suit from a hanger, and Leslie realized he was giving her a chance to cross the room in private.

Grateful, she slipped from the bed and padded to the bathroom door. After closing it behind her, she stepped into her dress and looked at herself in the mirror. Her cheeks were still flushed, and she smiled at her disheveled reflection. Something looked different, though she couldn't quite place what.

As she emerged from the bathroom, Grant handed her his card. "We live in Denver," he said. "Look us up if you're ever out our way. Like I said, I know Alicia would love to meet you too. If you were willing," he added in a tone that indicated he was aware of the relevance of such.

Leslie blushed and glanced at the business card he held out. "Thanks," she said. She looked back up at him.

Suddenly she felt to her core the freedom of this intimacy without uncertainty – the simplicity of connection, sexual, sincere, and affectionate, without the mess of "what happens now" concerns she usually associated with sex. She was startled to realize that this encounter, with a man who was married to someone else, might have encompassed the most open, authentic sex she'd ever had.

The irony stayed with her as she reflected on the way back to the party suite. She gathered her things, stepping over sleeping bodies as she made her way back to the hallway and took the elevator to the main floor.

The man, the room, the lavish environment surrounding her were all things she would have to leave, albeit with memories of considerable fondness. What she'd learned, though, what she'd seen as a result of an experience she'd never had before – that was hers to keep.

As she crossed the lobby and ventured into the bright new year that awaited her, she knew it was a tradeoff she was quite willing to make.

Of Her Own Accord

Evelyn's eyes roved the unfamiliar layout of an airport she'd never before been in. She glanced at a sign directing to ground transportation and followed the arrow, pulling her suitcase behind her as she watched for the rental car company with whom she'd made a reservation.

Though a couple hours from her destination, the airport here was cheaper than the one in the city where she was ultimately headed. Evelyn approached the car rental counter and moments later had signed the paperwork, accepted the keys, and was turning toward the door, a knot in her throat and nervous fluttering in her stomach. She was here now, two hours away from where the conference was, a full sixteen hours before it was scheduled to start. And she was staring down such a long shot that having even arranged to be in this position seemed suddenly and utterly absurd.

Evelyn took a deep breath and stepped forward and out the door. It was okay, she told herself. No one knew she was there, and it really was cheaper to fly to this airport – two hundred dollars cheaper, to be exact. If she didn't succeed in the mission she barely acknowledged was the reason for where she was, no one would ever know the difference.

She located the small red car in the parking lot and hauled her suitcase into the trunk. The muted thud of the car door as she closed it behind her sounded foreign, much smoother and sleeker than any sound her aged Honda made back home. She put the key in the ignition but didn't turn it.

She had no idea where to go.

She knew where the conference was. All she needed to do was exit the airport and follow the signs to the interstate that would take her right to the city with which she was familiar, where she had been numerous times on business in the last six years.

But she had all night. And she was here for a reason.

She'd had a dream about him three weeks before. It was a mesmerizing dream, one that somehow subverted reality, or at least compelled her enough that it had since been directing her attention, her fantasies, and, in some cases (like this one), her actions.

In high school, Robert Strickland's hair had been jet-black, his eyes dark crystal blue. Smooth fair skin and a sturdy build completed the solid, intimidating figure he cut in the black mesh football jersey and loose black jeans he wore on game days during their senior year. He'd been a hottie back then, as she recalled, but for whatever reason she hadn't noticed him much. Hardly at all, really.

Until the day her friend Lance, who was also on the football team, mentioned that he'd overheard Robert Strickland saying how much he wanted to fuck her.

Evelyn had felt quite surprised at the time. Though Robert was popular, almost darkly so with a bit of a notorious streak in his reputation, he also seemed unusually reserved for someone with such status. Rarely did she see him in conversation; to her he appeared an aloof figure whose mysterious, almost sinister air was perhaps the very spawn of his popularity. He had never spoken to her or so much as acknowledged her existence, and she had been truly unaware he even knew who she was.

After Lance's disclosure, Evelyn observed Robert covertly in the chemistry class they shared. He certainly hid his attraction well. He did not acknowledge her, and from simple observation, she still would have thought he didn't know she existed. She wondered if Lance had made a mistake.

Lance assured her, however, that Robert Strickland knew exactly who she was.

Evelyn had never felt compelled to act on the information Lance had imparted, but every once in a while she would recall it as she caught a glimpse of Robert's silent, enigmatic figure passing in the hall or rounding a corner out of sight. A distinct tug in the pit of her belly would follow, her pussy jumping to attention for an instant before her focus moved on to something else.

Maybe once in a while she had dressed in something a little lower cut on the days she had chemistry class.

She might have swung her hips a bit more when she walked by the table Robert shared with his lab partner. But that was all. And as far as she could see, he showed no response to any of it.

Throughout high school, she didn't remember speaking to him once.

The dream was set present-day, ten years after they'd all graduated and scattered like a handful of chicken feed from their small hometown. How the dream began, the fuzzy, disconnected details of the reunion gathering they'd seemed to be attending, of seeing Robert Strickland amongst the former high school football players in the room, were like the dream's introduction. Evelyn recalled them vaguely, and she could barely remember how they connected or exactly had led to the scene that followed.

It was that scene, the intoxicating, uninterrupted interaction between her and Robert Strickland responsible for countless orgasms since, that had cut through all the fogginess and nonexistence of a dream and seemed to penetrate reality itself, taking her breath as well as her attention away over and over again long after she had woken up. What replayed most vividly, more even than what he did or how he did it, were his words. How he spoke. What he said. It was that narration, the low string of unbroken utterances that permeated the entirety of the scene, whose magnetic intensity she had yet to escape.

"That's right, take that cock, you little slut. Spread those legs for me and take it hard and deep.

"You know we all used to talk about you in the locker room after football practice. How we wanted to shove our cocks in you, in your mouth, your pussy, your ass. Just like I'm doing now, ramming this big cock in your hot, tight pussy while you scream for more."

With the barking of each word, he slams his body against hers, shoving his cock balls-deep into her from behind.

"They'd all be so fucking jealous right now if they saw the way you were taking this cock and screaming for me. Would you like them all to be watching you right now, see them all pull their cocks out and jack off to your getting fucked hard like the filthy little whore you are?"

His touch is different from his words. As rough as it is, the actual physical contact from him feels fascinated, reverent, imbued with gratitude for the opportunity to touch her. She knows this is foundational to what he's doing – that he somehow knows he is giving her exactly what she craves.

"Or maybe you'd want them all to join me. Would you like that? You want all my football buddies to surround you with their cocks, shove one after another in your mouth while I fuck you from behind? You want us all to talk to each other about what a whore you are while we fuck you, shooting load after load of hot come all over your face?"

Evelyn shook herself, noticing she was slightly out of breath. Like her memory of Robert himself, the dream seemed dark, mysterious, intimate in an ominous way. While rife with sexual intensity, what was happening was not a fun, carefree romp. There was a seriousness to it, as though it touched a darkness within her that she hadn't been – may still not be – aware of.

She turned the key and shifted the rental car into gear, turning toward the airport exit. If the dream had intended to impart anything, she had no idea what it was. More than once she had felt compelled to remind herself – sternly – that it was a dream – it had no bearing on reality. But somehow, she had found the mirage magnetic, pulling her to the computer to look Robert Strickland up, finding nothing but the bare bones of his information on a social network site of which she wasn't a part, that listed only his name and his hometown and where he currently lived.

Which was here.

Evelyn comforted herself by acknowledging that had she discovered that Robert Strickland lived on the other side of the country from where her conference was, she would not have devised a plot to fly hours out of her way to land in the city where he lived for sixteen hours on the off chance she would somehow find him without looking like she was trying to find him. What she was doing was not entirely insane. She happened to save money flying into a nearby airport, and it happened to be in the city where she had just discovered Robert Strickland lived.

The long shot entered the picture, of course, with her complete ignorance of anything else about his whereabouts. She had no idea where he lived, where he worked, or even what line of work he was in. She had zero clue how to find him, and even if she did, she didn't want to appear to be looking for him. Showing up ten years after they'd last seen each other with the explanation that it was because of a dream she'd had was not a way she wanted to make an impression. Especially when they'd barely known each other back then.

Evelyn turned left out of the airport, heading downtown. She'd never even spoken to Robert Strickland. She didn't know what his voice sounded like. What would he be like in bed? Would that understated, almost ominously reserved demeanor segue into the low, menacing, rough sexual persona she – or at least her subconscious – imagined it would?

She bit her lip as the familiar suction of her attention began to possess her consciousness. It was like being underwater, except instead she was enveloped by the incessant, irrepressible, all-encompassing carnality this dream had released into her awareness. It took her concentration, melding it into a vortex-like opacity.

"Tight-bodied little whore. When I get done fucking your pussy, I'm going to shove this cock in your ass. Would you like that? Do you want to take it up the ass for me?" His voice turns to growls and moans at his own pleasure derived from her cunt. "That's right, baby, take this cock like the dirty little slut you are. I know what you want. And I'm going to give it to you all night." She is underneath him, face down on the bed as he jackhammers like a woodpecker above her, his rock-hard cock shoving its way in, deep, over and over and over again.

Evelyn blushed. She'd never had that kind of sex before – the kind in her dream, the kind that was playing out now in her head, with that kind of language and that kind of treatment. It was the intensity she felt from those words, and the sensations that resulted, that had still been with her when she'd woken up, breathless and sweating and so aroused she could barely see straight. Her hand had gone straight to her clit to complete the orgasm that had seemed to occur continuously as she dreamed.

Her pussy had been dripping. And Robert Strickland had been somewhere in her mind ever since.

Evelyn sat up straighter and redirected her attention as she began scanning the passing scenery for a place to eat. Even now her body seemed to be operating from this unseen place where her subconscious had concocted this scenario, the magnetism of this fantasy such that she was here, physically, in the city where Robert lived, thinking – what? That she'd drive around and somehow run into this mysterious, aloof jock from high school who had been rumored to want to fuck her yet never given any indication as such, and that he would give her exactly what she was looking for? Even if she did encounter him, would he even remember who she was?

He had certainly remembered in the dream.

A wood-paneled restaurant set back from the street caught Evelyn's attention, and she turned in and found a parking place. Switching off the engine, she unbuckled her seat belt and consciously resisted the urge to plunge her fingers into her drenched pussy.

Evelyn's mind, however, which seemed to be in cahoots with her cunt, appeared unwilling to be deterred. Stubbornly it returned to its familiar replay, to the connection it seemed to so easily make with the quiet, intense figure of Robert Strickland and a low voice whispering orders as she knelt in front of him, his strong fist clasping her hair in a sturdy grip:

"That's right, suck that cock, bitch. Good girl, suck it like a good little slut. Make me come all over your face like I know you want me to.

"I always knew you were a naughty girl. Even back in high school, before I'd ever spoken to you, I knew. I was right, wasn't I? You're a full-grown slut now, ready to take this cock I always wanted to plow into you."

Evelyn felt herself blushing furiously even as the vivid

scenario aroused her so much she felt almost dizzy. Her legs were shaking as she climbed from the car.

She avoided eye contact with the host as she asked for a table, afraid she might fuck anything with a dick until the adrenaline from her internal screenplay subsided. She followed him to a booth in the back and slipped quickly into it, accepting the menu as the host turned on his heel and disappeared. She could still feel the flush in her cheeks.

"Oh, yeah, I'm going to come in your mouth, bitch. Do you like that? You want my come all over your face?" He thrusts hard into her mouth, adding his other hand to the one already in her hair and fucking her face with abandon. "That's right, suck it deep."

"Any questions about the menu?"

"Uh – no, thank you," Evelyn stammered, feeling the challenge of yanking her concentration away from the explicit video reel in her head as she looked up at the server standing in front of her table.

She gave her order, barely aware of what she was requesting for dinner. As she waited, Evelyn felt her pussy dripping, her face burning as her food came and she did her best to eat like everyone else in the restaurant seemed to be, performing the relatively mundane act of consuming dinner rather than fantasizing about having the ever-loving shit fucked out of them by a former high school football-playing classmate. She reached under the table and pressed her clit for an instant, squirming uncomfortably at its screaming pressure for release.

Maybe she should just look him up and call him. He'd been interested back then – he'd understand if she said she wanted to fuck him, wouldn't he?

As the thought occurred to her, the true absurdity of

her position struck her like a slap. She had no idea what Robert Strickland's life was like, what he was doing now. He could be married for all she knew. The feeling was like being dropped to the ground from a blissful floating a few feet above it. She was in a city chasing a fantasy that, for all intents and purposes, had hijacked her consciousness. What, really, was she doing here? What did she really want?

Evelyn ran over her mental catalogue of past sexual partners. She would never have told any of them of the kind of fantasies she was having now. In fact, had it not been for the dream, she wasn't sure she would admit them to herself.

Yet right now, somehow, they felt like the only thing that would satisfy her.

Evelyn blushed, mortified even by the realization. Her subconscious was showing her things she wasn't sure she was ready to see.

For the first time it occurred to her to wonder – even if she encountered Robert, would she be able to ask him for what she was thinking? The dream had presented her with the ease of Robert's knowing what she wanted, giving it to her without hesitation or her having to say a word. And even now, awake and alert in this city where he lived, she realized she wanted that. She didn't want to say hi. She didn't care what he'd been up to for the last ten years. She didn't want any niceties at all.

All she wanted to hear from his mouth was filth.

Heat flooded her cheeks even as its presence increased in her belly. Why was he so compelling to her, this figure she had barely known when she was younger and who had seemed to signify something enigmatic and just out of reach even then?

It occurred to her that on some level, he had been out of reach at least partly of her own accord. The invitation had been there; it was she who hadn't acted on it. Had she preferred the mystery, the enigma to what might actually be? Or was it something more? Had she been avoiding something even then?

Was it – or did it represent – something she was avoiding now?

What she wanted now was dark and mysterious and ominous and unknown, but she wanted it almost anonymously, a moment of furtive and inconsequential rapture from which she could take what she wanted and go about her life.

And what did that mean? Wasn't wanting to satisfy this craving, however desperate it may seem, only with someone anonymous, someone with a mystique that seemed almost unreal, just short of not acknowledging it at all? Was that, ultimately, why the focus was on someone realistically so unreachable?

Frustrated and bewildered, Evelyn paid the check and slid from the booth. Even amidst her angst, the level of arousal in her made it difficult to walk, her pussy almost painfully swollen as she crossed the wooden floor of the restaurant and stepped outside, out to the city where Robert Strickland lived somewhere, possibly with a wife and kids and who knew what kind of life. Her eyes scanned the sidewalk and the opposite street in the twilight as she climbed into the rental car, her insides swishing with embarrassment that she was still looking for a shock of jet-black hair, the sturdy build of a high school football player.

Two and a half hours later, Evelyn checked into the high-end hotel where the conference was being held. Her eyes downcast, she accepted the keycard and slunk up to her room, dragging her luggage behind her.

It had been hard to drive away, to leave behind the city that seemed the only tangible link to what something inside her wanted so much. Twice she had felt forced to pull over and get herself off, the images in her mind continuing to swirl persistently. She wondered if Robert ever remembered her, had ever pictured her when he jerked himself off. Had the vision of her ever similarly captivated him?

At her room, she slid the card into the slot and walked into the darkness. The door closed behind her, and she let out a deep breath. For some reason she felt exhausted.

Leaving her suitcase in the entryway, she moved to the bed and barely managed to get her clothes off before she fell into it. Even as her eyes closed, her hand slid covertly to her clit.

"What a horny little slut you are. I always knew what a cock-whore you were, how much you wanted to be held down and have a big cock shoved into you over and over again, just like this. That's right, Evelyn, take that cock. Take it like the slutty little whore you are."

Evelyn woke up an hour later. Not bothering to rise from the bed, she stared silently at the understated stripes on the curtains over the large window. She lay there, not moving, not sleeping, for almost another hour before she rose quietly and slipped back into her clothes.

Exiting the room, she took the elevator down to the lobby and crossed the marble floor to the concierge.

"Hi, could I make a spa appointment for tomorrow

morning, please?" Evelyn tried to sound like she knew what she was doing, when in reality she had never indulged in such a thing as spa time.

She was unaware, still, of any message the dream was meant to convey. But for the last hour as she'd just let herself sit with it, nowhere else to go, nothing else to do, she'd sensed in it somehow a mysterious underlying mandate – a mandate to pay attention to matters of something inside her besides obligation, responsibility, what she perpetually felt was expected of her. Matters, simply, of what she wanted.

Wanted. Even the word seemed foreign to her. It was something she hadn't paid attention to in a long time. Possibly, she realized with a pang, ever.

Raising her eyes, she resisted the urge to turn and run back to her room and steeled herself to follow that want, to follow, just like she had the vision of the dream, what it felt like, the inexpressible desire that led to the body, the imagination, connection, pleasure.

All things of which she was startled to realize her own neglect.

The elegant receptionist smiled at her. "Of course," she answered, turning to her computer. "Let me see what's available." Evelyn studied the woman's relaxed, open expression from beneath lowered lashes as she clicked away at the keyboard. "What kind of service would you like? I have an opening for a facial at 8:00 tomorrow morning. Or a massage at 11:00... let's see, a full-body wrap at 10:30." She turned her dark eyes back to Evelyn, who blushed a little at the woman's slow smile, which struck her somehow as provocative. "Would any of those work for you?"

Evelyn hesitated for a split second. She would be expected, she was sure, to report in the morning by eight o'clock, focusing for the hour before the conference began on any last-minute preparations. It wasn't required – check-in didn't start until nine. But she wouldn't be expected at eight because it was required. She would be expected then because it was what she'd always done.

She met the knowing brown eyes of the receptionist and felt the physical jolt of recollection tug through her body. With a shy smile she said, "Yes. I'll take the eight o'clock, please."

The receptionist winked and gave a tiny nod as she turned back to the computer. Evelyn watched as sparkling manicured fingers typed in the name she recited before filling out an appointment card and handing it to her. She accepted it, looking down at the shiny black ink announcing her name.

It wasn't the kind of facial she wanted. But maybe right now, it was the kind she needed.

Wherever Robert Strickland was, she dedicated it to him.

Lifeline

Chelsea scrubbed her fingers with a nail brush, trying to erase the inevitable grime of working at Carter's Auto Service. Yawning, she rinsed her hands, their cleanliness reaching the peak of where it was going to get, and returned to her bedroom.

She sat down at the vanity and uncapped the tiny bottle of nail glue. Carefully she brushed her left thumb with the miniature applicator and picked up the first of ten artificial nails arranged on the glass in front of her. She pressed it into place, glancing at the clock as she held it for several seconds to let the glue dry.

When her nails were applied, all but obliterating any evidence of the grunge of her day job, Chelsea located her heels and dropped them in her bag. Rummaging through her wardrobe to find what she would wear that night, she pulled out a minuscule tube dress and stuffed it into the bag as well, threw her curling iron in on top of it, and grabbed her purse on the way out the door.

The parking lot of the Silver Dollar, which didn't open for another half hour, was mostly empty as she pulled in. Chelsea parked near the entrance and grabbed her gear from the front seat. Making her way to the opaque door that had become familiar over the last three months, she pushed through it without pausing, thus making the transition from Cheslea to Mickey.

She saw Jocelyn right away. Chelsea's nerves began to tingle like vibrating cello strings as Jocelyn caught sight of her and headed her way with a smile.

"Mickey!" The warm greeting, filled with affection Chelsea knew was strictly friendly, made Chelsea's nerves vibrate harder nonetheless. Jocelyn wrapped her in a hug, then let go to ask Chelsea how she was. Her dark eyes offered the undivided attention that made her one of the most consistently successful dancers at the club. Which happened, Chelsea knew, without Jocelyn's even trying. Jocelyn loved her job, for sure, but she also loved people, which was what Chelsea felt made people, including customers, love her so much back.

She, of course, loved Jocelyn more than most. As per usual, Chelsea squirmed internally at the intensity of the attraction and the knowledge that no one, with the exception of her friend Alex, knew about it, including the target of the infatuation herself.

It had been three months since Chelsea had started dancing at the Silver Dollar, three months since her mother had told her of her illness and Chelsea had been made aware that the medical bills that were going to start coming would be well beyond what her mother could afford. Chelsea remembered the first day she'd walked into the club and met Jocelyn's dark chocolate eyes –

eyes that managed to make the goddess-like mocha body below them take second place, commanding all attention into their rich depths until they took it upon themselves to relinquish it.

On the stage, Jocelyn was almost beyond comprehension. With seamless elegance she would run her long nails up her smooth, dark skin, her black hair swirling into big curls at her shoulders. Her deep brown eyes missed no one as she ran them around the stage below her. When she smiled, usually looking from under her lashes in a pose rife with both coyness and allure, her teeth positively glimmered against the background of her magnificent ebony skin. She was beautiful.

Of course, most of Chelsea's co-workers were beautiful. Even Chelsea herself had been told she was beautiful – here, anyway. It wasn't a compliment she recalled hearing much anywhere else.

But most of her co-workers weren't Jocelyn. Chelsea took a deep breath as she went to the dressing room to prepare for her set. She wondered as she brushed her blonde hair if it would be easier if she didn't see Jocelyn all the time – naked, no less. Much as she admired Jocelyn from afar, Chelsea had to endure interacting with her as a friend too, the other woman's exquisite blend of innocence and awareness making her unbearably appealing while reducing Chelsea to what felt like a puddle of mindlessness.

Despite their friendship, Chelsea had no idea if Jocelyn was interested in women. Working up the nerve to approach someone she had a crush on had always been challenging for Chelsea, and the addition of the unorthodox twist of having to discern "orientation," as it were, had generally tossed the idea so far out of her comfort zone it may as well have landed on another continent.

She had a feeling, though, that Jocelyn was no stranger to such liaisons. Her co-worker seemed to exhibit no inhibitions, nothing but grace and curiosity and openness, somehow maintaining what seemed an utmost sincerity in this world thought to be so full of falsity and manipulation. It was obvious Jocelyn loved the men to whom she catered professionally; but really, Chelsea reflected, Jocelyn seemed to love everybody.

"Mickey" was announced, and Chelsea descended the stairs from the dressing room to the stage. Like metal to a magnet, her eyes found Jocelyn instantly in the crowd. She was near the bar in the back, speaking with a well-dressed gentleman who stood up as Chelsea watched, stepping back to let Jocelyn lead him toward the VIP area.

Jocelyn turned her head toward the stage. Chelsea felt a jolt zip through her as her friend's eyes met hers, followed instantly by that brilliant snow-white smile Jocelyn never seemed to hold back. She winked and blew Chelsea a kiss just before she disappeared through the doorway of the VIP lounge.

Chelsea worked to catch her breath. She had wondered sometimes if her infatuation inadvertently helped her with business. Potential customers may not know the cause of the flush on her cheeks or the shimmer of moisture on her naked pussy as she twirled around the pole. But they may appreciate them nonetheless – never knowing they were the result of the stunning woman making the rounds in her trademark white seven-inch heels, the aura of perfection Chelsea saw in her emanating like a cloud of perfume.

As Chelsea dipped low now, focusing her gaze on the circle of customers surrounding the stage, she felt the blood rushing to her clit – but it wasn't because of the excitement of the spotlight or the men looking hungrily at her from the front row and back as far as the bar to the side of the stage. It was because of that kiss, the innocent gesture Jocelyn had undoubtedly offered with the same casualness she had her smile but that sent Chelsea's imagination into places wet with desire. Her mind whirled with images of Jocelyn's stunning dark hair thrown back as she thrust her bare breasts toward Chelsea's mouth, of Chelsea's fingers plunging deep into the hot recesses of her desire, her body – her soul.

A scattering of applause startled her from her reverie as her first song ended. Flushed and out of breath, she found herself in a position she didn't remember getting into, on her knees with her thighs splayed wide, her hands gripping her breasts. She could feel that her royal blue g-string was almost soaked through.

With a deep breath, she stood somewhat unsteadily and began her second song.

Alex pushed a drawer of the metal toolbox shut with a clang. "Want to grab dinner after we close?" he called to her across the service bay.

Chelsea finished replacing the distributor cap of the SUV whose hood she was under. "I have to work tonight," she grumbled. She must be one of the only people in the greater metropolitan area who disliked Fridays. Working both her jobs that day made it not one she tended to look forward to. "Which means in three hours I have to look like a model ready for a photo spread – as much as I can, anyway." Chelsea glowered at the SUV's engine, aware of the grease smeared on her sweat-covered neck and, as usual when she was at the shop, caked under her nails and covering her hands.

"Well, right now you're a great big mess," Alex said cheerfully.

"Yeah, thanks," Chelsea muttered, emerging from under the hood and grabbing the rag from her back pocket. Knowing that Jocelyn wasn't working that night pretty much eliminated all appeal of the prospect of going to work for another several hours after she got done at Carter's.

Alex had the rough, scruffy, dirty-blond look so many bad-boy fantasies seemed to be made of. Usually sporting a few days' beard, his hair sexily unkempt and just long enough to reach his eyes, the grease customarily smeared over his coveralls or the white t-shit he wore underneath completed the look. Chelsea had seen more than one woman linger a little longer than necessary as Alex went to work on her vehicle, running her eyes up and down his flawless physique and seeking, Chelsea suspected, another kind of service altogether.

"Where's Caroline tonight?" she asked, remembering Alex's invitation.

Alex turned away and walked back to the toolbox, stuffing his own rag in his pocket as he went. He didn't answer right away.

"She went to her parents' for the weekend."

Chelsea sent him a glance before picking up a wrench and returning to the SUV's engine. The volatile nature of

Alex and Caroline's five-year relationship had culminated in what had seemed to be a constant on-again, off-again pattern for the last two. Chelsea surmised that they were probably in the midst of another one of their extended arguments.

"Well, I'm sorry I'm not available tonight," she said into the grime inches from her face. "I could do lunch tomorrow if you want."

"How's your mom doing?" Alex's voice came again.

Chelsea sighed. "Good question." The inquiry reminded her that she was probably overdue for a phone call to her mother, another thing she didn't look forward to. Tossing her wrench on the floor, Chelsea stood up and wiped her hands before lowering the hood of the SUV, watching as it fell closed with a thud.

Chelsea slept in the next day. She wasn't working at Carter's, and she didn't have to go to the Silver Dollar until evening. After making French toast for breakfast, she made her way back into the bedroom, flopped on the bed, and stared at the phone.

Without thinking enough to change her mind, she reached for it and punched in the number. As she listened to the ringing on the other end, her stomach suddenly swirled with sadness, and she found it hard to speak through the lump in her throat when her mother answered.

"Hi, Mom."

"Hello, Chelsea."

Chelsea repositioned herself on the bed, sitting up and bringing her legs toward her as she leaned back against the pillows.

"How are you feeling?" Chelsea's eyes dropped to the streaks of sunlight the open blinds stenciled across the floor as she listened to the dry response informing her that her mother felt tired and not much was different.

"But there's no reason to worry about me so much. I'll be fine."

Cheslea restrained a sigh. She was well aware that what that meant was that her mother felt neglected and was considering embarking on one of her famous guilt trips. Chelsea tried to recall the last conversation she'd had with her mother that didn't include one of these.

Her mother was still talking. "So anyway, it's just another test, and it probably won't tell him anything different than any of the other ones have."

"Yeah, but it's a good idea to listen to your doctor, Mom. I'm sure he knows what he's doing."

"Ha! Yeah, I'm sure he makes a lot of money knowing what he's doing, too. This test alone'll cost $200. He must think the salary of a secretary is generous or something."

Chelsea closed her eyes briefly. "Mom, you know I'm helping you with your medical bills. Do what your doctor says."

There was a brief silence, and Chelsea narrowed her eyes as she sensed her mother's embarrassment. While she was usually pretty straightforward about accepting money – she thought it was an even trade after she worked so hard to raise Chelsea all by herself – sometimes it seemed to humble her.

"Mom?"

"Yes. Yes, I know that, Chelsea, and I appreciate it. This is all just such a nuisance. But I suppose I brought it on myself, running all those years trying to raise you without taking any time to take care of myself."

Chelsea looked at the ceiling. "I'll send you a check next weekend, Mom."

At the club that night, the conversation returned to her. Even at twenty-four, seven years after she had hightailed it out of her mother's house at age seventeen, Chelsea still sometimes felt like the little girl who could never seem to do what was needed to make her mother happy. Her mother had been one big mesh of ignoring and smothering throughout her childhood, swinging back and forth between the two like a pendulum on a clock Chelsea never learned how to read. Early on Chelsea had stopped resenting the fact that she didn't have a father and focused on trying to elude her mother, who had managed to remind her constantly how hard it was to be a single parent, as if Chelsea had somehow asked to be born into the circumstance she was and held single-handed responsibility for the difficulty her mother perceived in her life.

The day Chelsea had found her mother in the kitchen to share the news that she'd gotten her first period, the response she'd received was, "I hope you don't think that means you're old enough to start having sex. Because if you ever get pregnant while you're living under my roof, you won't be living under it anymore." Her mother had emphasized the words with a sharp thrust of the knife into the block of cheddar she'd been slicing while Chelsea had stood stock-still, too stunned and mortified to say a word.

Chelsea wasn't prone to hilarity, but she chuckled dryly to herself now as she walked through the club, thinking about the clueless 12-year-old girl she'd been and how ironic it was that she was a stripper now. It would be a few years after that yet that she'd learn much about sex – before she started having it, but after she realized the interest she felt in girls as well as boys was not universal – to say the least – and begun the process of grappling with that in the context of the small rural town where they lived. Had it not been for the blessedly open-minded mother of her best friend in high school, Chelsea had no idea how she would have traversed any of it. Especially since despite her mother's dire warnings – which would from then on become a theme filled with grave threats but no concrete information to speak of – the woman never gave her any information about birth control. It was thanks to Vanessa's mom that Chelsea had gotten on the pill before she needed to be and that she carried condoms in her purse to this day.

Not that she'd needed them much in recent years. Another irony. She was a stripper who hadn't had sex in six months.

A prospective customer caught her eye, and Chelsea shook her thoughts aside, giving him a smile as she started across the room and returned her attention to her job.

Chelsea did a double take as she noticed the lights on at the shop on her way home. She switched lanes and turned into the parking lot, spotting Alex's truck parked behind the building.

The door was locked, and Chelsea flipped through her keys and let herself in. She walked through the reception area back to the office.

"What are you doing here?" she asked Alex, who was sitting on the floor of the bay just beyond the office door, a beer in his hand.

He looked up. Chelsea couldn't tell if he was surprised to see her or not. He didn't answer, and Chelsea sat down on the concrete floor beside him.

Alex stared straight ahead. "Caroline came back tonight." He took a swig of his beer and paused for so long Chelsea was about to respond when he said, "She said it was just to get her stuff."

Chelsea lowered her head. She reached to rest her fingertips on the sleeve of Alex's t-shirt. "You two have worked things out before, Alex. She probably just wants some time to cool off."

"Nah... I think it's really done this time." Alex's voice held just enough restraint of the desolation Chelsea sensed at its base that suddenly, she knew he was right. The automatic words of encouragement she'd been about to offer died on her lips.

They sat silently for several moments. Chelsea looked at Alex as he took another swig. In profile, what looked like the sheen of tears covered his eyes as he lowered the bottle, and she reached and squeezed his shoulder, letting her hand rest there for several seconds.

After a while Alex hoisted his body up from the concrete. "Anyway, I should get home and start sorting things out." He wiped his hands on his jeans and looked down at her.

Chelsea didn't know if he meant literally as far as the items in his and Caroline's shared apartment or something less tangible. She stood as well, brushing off her skirt as she killed the bay lights and followed him into the office.

"Call me if you need anything," she said as he picked up his keys.

Alex turned and kissed her. There was no question in it, no introduction, no hesitance, yet no possessiveness, no demand, either. She wasn't even sure if he himself had anticipated it any more than she had. He kissed her with the same immediacy with which she returned it, neither of them, she suspected, really thinking about it at all – just doing, something borne of the moment neither of them had the energy to question or strong enough desire to resist.

Alex grabbed her, squeezing her body like a lifeline, turning and pulling her on top of him as he sat in the swivel chair, their kiss never breaking. The urgency Chelsea felt in Alex's actions wasn't about her, she knew, and there was an honesty in that, a vulnerability she found herself touched by. It was what he needed, and something about that pulled in her even as her body began to respond beyond anything her mind might have to say.

Her skirt came up, and Alex plunged his fingers into her. Chelsea's breath disappeared, abandon securing a sudden and unforeseen possession of her as Alex tore off her shirt and she held on to his in desperation, a wetness that surprised her spilling onto Alex's fingers as he touched her clit lightly with his thumb.

Maybe it was what they both needed.

She looked down and met his eyes, fierce in the darkness as he gripped her waist and pulled her tighter against him. Reaching between their bodies, she felt the hardness beneath his jeans and twisted away to pull open her purse on the desk. She snatched the long-neglected condom from its home in the front pocket, and Alex took it from her and ripped it open as she stood to give him room.

For a second, there was a pause. She stood above him, looking into his shining eyes in the muted darkness of the office. Alex breathed heavily, his gaze never leaving hers as they stared, suspended, in the eye of the hurricane for this instant undefined.

Then their lips were joined again, her body dropping onto his as Alex's fingers dug into her hips. She rode him frantically, his thumb back on her clit as her hands found their way to his hair and clutched desperate fistfuls as she started to come with a long, crescendoing moan she didn't recognize as coming from her. Alex gripped her harder, a strangled sound tearing from his own throat. The pain it held evoked Chelsea's own as they hung on to each other through climax, the moment agony and ecstasy blended into one, surpassing all identity into pure being, reminding them only that they were alive – and that that was all they needed.

Neither of them moved as the descent began, heartbeats slowing and breaths evening. Chelsea's eyes were closed against Alex's neck as she felt the reorientation to the mundane begin to infiltrate her consciousness. But as she stood, she felt the looseness of her body, a relaxation she couldn't remember the last time she'd experienced. Her breathing came literally easier as she exhaled the last of what had just been released and aligned involuntarily with a new groundedness her body seemed to possess.

Chelsea turned in the darkness to give Alex a hug and caught her breath when she felt, rather than saw, a similar alchemical energy in his eyes. What it meant for him she couldn't know, but she was aware beyond doubt that it could only be enriching.

Alex closed the door behind them as they stepped into the night. The air felt lighter than she remembered.

Open Invitation

The expected knock came at the door, and Gina clicked the "break" button on the computer screen and ran from the bedroom to answer it. The apartment complex was having renovations to each individual apartment done, and she had received written notice a few days ago that the contractors would be starting on her building this week.

She pulled the door open. A young man with roguish blue eyes and a blond goatee stood in a customary dark blue maintenance uniform. His eyes flicked up and down Gina's short black satin robe and bare legs, and he grinned.

"Hi," he said, his jaw flexing as he shifted the gum in his mouth. "I'm here to install the new thermostat in your apartment."

"Of course," Gina said, stepping back to let him in. "Come in."

He stepped past her, loaded down with tools and

equipment, and Gina returned the once-over he'd bestowed upon her as he walked across the living room. She closed the door.

"So you live here by yourself?" he began conversationally as he unlocked the utility closet at the far side of the room.

"Yes. I'm actually working right now, so I'm about to get back to that. I'm Gina, by the way. Is everything moved out of your way?"

He turned from the utility closet and looked her up and down again. "Yeah, no problem. I'm Ben. You work at home?"

"I do," she said briskly. She didn't mind conversing, but she was still on the clock and needed to get back to work.

"What do you do?"

"I'm a webcam model." Ben turned and stared at her, and Gina smiled. It wasn't unusual for people to seem surprised when she disclosed her line of work – some seemed to expect her to want to keep it a secret or something – and she was usually glad to field questions, but she had to get back to work. "I have to run now, though. Thanks," she called over her shoulder as she headed down the hallway.

Ben was cute – temptingly so. A few years ago she would likely have already hit on him and preferably been mid-fuck by now. But that was then. Gina turned her focus back to work, choosing to not dwell on any of the other reasons she might not be interested in engaging with Ben right now.

She closed the bedroom door and re-donned the silver negligee and g-string she was working in. Stepping back into her heels, she reached for the laptop and clicked the "break" button again, turning the webcam and microphone back on.

A list of viewers came up in the box next to her cam view, and she laughed and chatted flirtatiously until the "Private" indicator came on, indicating someone had paid for a show.

It was screen name "doug1763," one of her regulars, and she smiled. Doug knew just what she liked, and vice versa. Gina greeted him and lay back against the pillows, running a hand slowly down the satin covering her body. She winked at the camera before flicking her eyes to the response he typed in the text box.

She flipped over and rose to her knees, peeling off her negligee with her ass to the camera. Looking back over her shoulder, Gina giggled at the approving message on the screen. She shook her ass a bit and turned back around. Doug started typing dirty, which he knew she loved, as Gina spread her legs and dropped her hand between them. She watched the screen as he called her a slut and a dirty whore and told her to get on her knees and suck him off. Gina moaned and worked her clit expertly.

She soon came with a scream reading Doug's "Suck my cock, you dirty little slut" message, and as she caught her breath, she smiled into the camera. Doug typed a message of characteristic flattery, and she said out loud, "Ready to see it again?"

Gina reached down and fingered her cunt again, bringing forth another orgasm in about a minute. This time she squirted, as she did the next a few minutes later. She looked at the text box and smiled at Doug's enthusiastic description of his own orgasm. He thanked her, and Gina smiled and waved as he signed out, then pulled her g-string and negligee back on before her cam returned to the public viewing area.

Two more shows came in quick succession. Both were with new customers, and Gina chatted and laughed and stripped and came for each. Though each show she did was different, ultimately Gina knew exactly how to produce what her customers were paying to see. Sometimes they contributed to her enjoyment, but she was well versed in inducing what her job called for even if such stimulation was absent. She knew well how to make herself come and exactly when it was going to happen. If she wanted to slow it down, she could; if she wanted to come quickly, no problem. Gina had long ago mastered the art of self-induced orgasm.

She glanced at the clock as a show ended and saw that her shift was up. Gina blew a kiss to the camera as she announced her imminent departure to the public viewers and logged out.

She grabbed her robe in case any of the renovations crew was still in her apartment and emerged from the bedroom. When she entered the living room she saw that Ben was indeed still there, kneeling in front of the furnace wielding a wrench and covered in dust. He heard her and turned.

"Hi there. Still working?"

"No, done for the day," Gina answered.

Ben nodded, giving his gum a slow chomp as his eyes ran down her legs. He turned back to the furnace. "Good day?"

"Not bad," she said.

"Sounded like you were having fun."

"Oh, you could hear me?" Gina flushed a bit.

Ben turned back to her. "Uh, yeah."

Gina laughed a bit self-consciously at his impish tone. "I work with a mic, so sound is included in my shows. It thus isn't always quiet."

Ben pocketed his wrench. As he passed by to examine the thermostat, he glanced her way and said, "Something tells me it wouldn't be very quiet whether you worked with a mic or not."

Gina blinked, surprised by his directness. She noticed also that it turned her on and recalled quickly that she wasn't looking for any such involvement right now. She and Jeff had only broken up three weeks ago, and she didn't feel at all interested yet in getting otherwise involved. A casual fuck was one thing, but frankly the breakup had been intense, and Gina wasn't even sure she felt up to that right now.

Silently she sent this reminder to her pussy, which seemed to have forgotten.

"Is that your boyfriend in the pictures over there?"

Gina looked up, startled by the relation of the question to her thoughts. Ben nodded at the pictures in question. Her eyes followed, and she was silent for a moment. When she didn't answer, Ben gave her a glance over his shoulder.

"No," she said. Ben continued to look at her. "Recent ex." Gina stood up, ready to drop the subject. "I'm going to take a shower," she said, effectively closing the conversation. "You don't need anything from me, do you?"

Ben flicked his gaze over her body and up to her eyes. After a slight pause that Gina knew was deliberate, he said with a sly smile, "Nope. Go right ahead."

Gina scurried away from his twinkling blue eyes and shut the bathroom door behind her. Her thoughts were on Jeff as she dropped her robe and lingerie to the floor, feeling the pull of sadness as she turned on the shower. They were through, she knew, and she was perfectly free to do whatever she wanted. But fucking someone else felt like a finality somehow, an acknowledgment that she and Jeff were really done. It was an acknowledgment she didn't quite feel ready for yet.

Gina stepped into the shower, melancholy washing over her like the steady rush of warm water. She breathed deeply, taking in the soothing eucalyptus and peppermint scent of her body wash, and took her time running her soapy hands over her skin. When she finally turned off the tap, Gina guessed Ben and any other of the maintenance crew would be gone, though she had no idea how long the renovations were supposed to take. Just in case, she wrapped a towel around herself before opening the door.

Ben stood in the hallway, examining the fuse box.

"Oh – excuse me," she said in surprise.

He turned to her. "Excuse me." Gallantly he stepped aside, and Gina caught her breath as she slid past him to the bedroom. He made no secret of checking her out as she did.

Gina frowned internally at the insistent response from her pussy. Flustered, she crossed the threshold and shut the bedroom door. It was funny – back when she would have jumped Ben without hesitation, she wouldn't have felt shy or embarrassed at all in this situation. It was as though *not* initiating sex felt awkward to her. What did one do instead in the face of such attraction and no clear reason not to act on it?

Gina put her clothes on with a certain firmness, as though they served as literally another layer of self-control. When she reemerged from the bedroom, Ben was back in the living room, crouching in front of the utility closet.

He gave his screwdriver a twirl. Gina studied him, wondering how old he was. She would guess mid-twenties. She smiled to herself as she remembered her own mid-twenties and imagined how thrilled she would have been then with an opportunity like Ben showing up at her door.

Ben stood up and returned to the thermostat. He tinkered with it for a bit and returned to the furnace as she watched him.

"You're my last apartment today," he commented.

"You don't say." Gina pulled her concentration back to the present.

"Yep. I get off at four."

Gina took a deep breath as he stood up and turned back to her, leaning against the wall and folding his arms.

"So what are you doing tonight after I get off work?"

Gina laughed politely. "Ben," she started. She paused. "You know, it's funny. A few years ago, I can assure you I would have hit on you already. While being cognizant of the fact that you were working, of course, and not wanting you to feel uncomfortable, I would have asked you to fuck me the second you were done with whatever it is you're doing with that thermostat there."

Ben's gaze penetrated hers. "I wouldn't feel un-comfortable."

Gina smiled and looked down.

He continued. "So why aren't you doing that now?"

"Things are different now."

"Then why'd you mention it?"

The question caught her off guard. Gina looked up and met Ben's teasing expression.

"I don't know. Why not?"

"I just wonder why you'd say something like that if you weren't thinking you wanted it now."

Gina noted to herself that she had said nothing about not actually wanting it now. Mercifully, she managed to bite her tongue before that slipped out of her mouth into the room.

Ben turned to put some things back together on the furnace as she remained silent. Then he closed and locked the utility closet.

"All finished," he said with a wink. His gaze locked with hers as he stood for a moment before beginning to gather his tools.

Gina noticed she was a little out of breath. She cleared her throat. "Well, thanks," she said. "It was nice meeting you."

Ben finished collecting his equipment and walked to within a foot of her. His blue eyes shot into hers like lasers. Gina nearly trembled at his proximity as heat fired in her core, threatening to physically push her closer to him. She swallowed.

He spoke. "I'm off work as soon as I walk out of here. You want me to come back up here and fuck you after I drop everything off?"

Gina's legs seemed to melt a little beneath her. She had almost forgotten why she would possibly say no to such an offer. Her body was going against her, its unreserved interest pulsating from her pussy as she stared at him.

"Uh – " she almost panicked, aware that Ben would use any hesitation he sensed in pursuit of what he was after. She gathered herself and cleared her throat. "No, thank you," she said, smiling. "But I appreciate your asking. Have a good day."

Ben's mischievous eyes gave her one more once-over as he took a step back and smiled. "I'll be finishing the rest of your floor tomorrow. Let me know if you change your mind."

Gina swallowed again and led him to the door, waving goodbye and locking it firmly behind him.

She wasn't working the next day, and Gina found herself recalling with inconvenient frequency that Ben was somewhere on her floor throughout the day. Late in the afternoon she decided to go to the store. At just past 4:00 p.m. she grabbed her keys and yanked open the door, telling herself she wasn't leaving at this particular time because she was trying to run into Ben. She just needed to go to the store.

As she inserted the key to lock the door behind her, she froze as an arm suddenly snaked around her waist from behind.

"Looking for me?" The voice was low, but the pressure of him from behind was far from subtle. Gina caught her breath as her body responded beyond her control to the feel of his hot breath against her skin. She didn't answer.

Ben's quiet voice continued in her ear. "I think maybe you were. I'd bet you're just about ready to admit how much you want to be fucked hard. You probably knew

67

how much I wanted to fuck you all day yesterday when you were in your bedroom naked and screaming and coming over and over again, knowing I was in the next room listening with a hard cock and holding myself back from barging in there and fucking you right then."

Despite her physical response, some of Gina's resolve returned. "What if I say no?" The truth was that word was nowhere near what she wanted to say, but she felt like rebelling a little against his aggressiveness. She really was curious what he would say if she continued to put him off.

"Then you say no. But I don't think you want to." Ben's hand pushed between their bodies and squeezed her ass as he dipped his head and bit her earlobe ever so lightly. Gina sucked in a breath. She jammed the key in the door, her body making the decision for her. At this point she felt beyond no.

Ben closed the door behind them, already pulling at her shirt. Gina shrugged it the rest of the way off as he gripped her hair kissed her neck roughly, nudging her toward the bedroom. Their clothes were off by the time they reached it.

"This time when I hear you scream, it's going to be because of me," Ben hissed in her ear as he shoved her onto the bed. Gina caught her breath as he pushed on top of her, kissing her aggressively. He ran a hand roughly through her hair, and Gina knew she was so wet she could take him easily right then. Automatically she moved her hand to her pussy.

Ben grabbed her wrist. Her eyes were closed, and they opened at the force of his grip.

"No way," Ben said. "You're not doing it to yourself now.

I'm the one that gets to have that fun."

Gina blinked. She couldn't remember the last time she had had an orgasm unassisted by herself. She and Jeff hadn't had sex much the last several months they'd been together, and when they had he had usually seemed content to let Gina take care of herself. Of course, she certainly wasn't short on getting off and hadn't particularly felt she was missing out. What difference did it make whether she did it to herself or not?

Ben shoved her up on the bed and moved down between her legs. Gina almost laughed. It had been so long since someone had gone down on her it seemed like some sort of absurd luxury, and she almost stopped him.

As she started to speak, however, Ben looked up at her, and she saw in the hard look in his eyes that he wasn't open to argument. Gina felt the responsive heat low in her belly and dropped her head back as Ben dove into her pussy and started licking. He used his tongue solidly, and within moments Gina was so turned on she felt almost lightheaded. She was ready to come, and unconsciously her hand slid across her thigh toward her pussy.

Her attention was abruptly jolted when she felt Ben's not-so-gentle grip around her wrist again. "Sweetheart, I'll tie you up if I have to." The voice matched the feel of his grip. "This isn't your job this time. Your pussy's mine until I'm done with it. Got it?"

The words made her shiver as arousal shot straight to the referenced part of her anatomy. Ben gripped her hips and worked his tongue tirelessly, her body twisting and shoving and trying to manipulate. She was past wanting to come and knew she could make her herself do so in seconds. As she squirmed, Ben held her hips and lifted his head to give her a look. She realized as she met his steel gaze that he wasn't going to let her help at all.

With a sigh, Gina leaned back and rested her arms above her head on the pillow in an effort to keep them from unthinkingly straying again. Then she took a deep breath, consciously dropped all effort, and let him take over.

It felt strange as her body relaxed. Almost immediately a tension she hadn't known was there seemed to release. The sensation of pleasure in her clit magnified.

"Oh," she said. Gina's eyes widened as her experience shifted right in front of her. She didn't have to work at anything – performance was not her responsibility right now. The sensation in her body expanded as though from a narrow, focused laser to a sheet of shimmering bliss covering her entire form.

Another soft moan slipped from her throat. She had all but forgotten that sensation – not coming and not trying to come. Just pure stimulation.

Gina breathed deeply and cried out suddenly as she came, her eyes widening as she realized she hadn't even known she was going to. Her wails pulsated as her body contracted beyond her control, Ben's tongue still on her clitoris as she gripped the pillow above her head.

Her fingers loosened as the climax receded, her body pinging with ecstatic energy. Ben rose to his knees and gave her a little smile.

"That's better," he said as he reached for his pants, pulling a condom out of the back pocket. He ripped it open and rolled it over his cock as Gina lay still, breathless and incoherent.

Positioning himself above her, Ben rammed into her

without preamble. Gina screamed as fire exploded in her core. He pounded and she took it gleefully, a feeling of euphoria overtaking her in the face of this relinquishment of all control, even over her own pleasure. She almost laughed as she wondered when that feeling had become so foreign.

Ben pulled out and turned her over, and Gina rose eagerly to her hands and knees as he reached under her and pressed his fingers against her clit while he took her from behind. Gina came again without warning, screaming ecstatically as Ben gripped her shoulder and slammed into her, grunting soon as he climaxed himself.

Gina dropped forward onto the bed and rolled over, sweating, panting, and seeing stars. Ben's grin was impish as he winked at her and hoisted himself off the bed. As he located his clothes, Gina caught her breath, her vision still a bit fuzzy.

"Thanks," she finally managed.

Ben grinned again. "My pleasure." He pulled her up and looked her up and down as she stood before him, naked. "I'm glad I got to take over your job for the day."

Gina's laugh was breathless. "Yeah," she agreed as she watched him buckle his belt. Her laughter faded as her attention moved inward. She was barely aware of speaking out loud when she said, "Me too."

After a moment her face cleared, and Gina smiled at him. "It was certainly a memorable day off."

Ben finished dressing and gave her a now-familiar once-over before meeting her eyes. "Well, I'll be working in your building for at least the next two weeks." His cobalt gaze penetrated hers. "Consider it an open invitation."

Is Not Gold

"OCTOBER," the bold letters of the calendar announced. Unmoving, unfeeling, they stared blandly at her with no notion of what they represented for her. The smooth, shiny paper hung motionless on the wall, a direct contrast to what it exacerbated in her.

She looked to the date circled in blue. For weeks she'd been watching it, watching with an ache that spread as the number of squares between the current day and that blue circle became fewer and fewer. Today there were no squares left. It was down to a matter of hours.

"I was just thinking about the time when I was ten. And my cat died. He got run over." She spoke tonelessly, staring at the far-off horizon below the hazy sky. The sun and clouds had reached a standoff, medium orange rays giving way to creeping gray that was in turn subverted again.

He looked over at her. "What made you think of that?"

She shrugged, not breaking her gaze. "I have no idea. I just did."

He turned back to face the horizon with her. The water not more than twenty yards in front of them reflected the orange rays and gray cloud mass in turn. A crow cried from what sounded like far off, though when he looked up he spotted it swooping toward the top of one of the tall pine trees not far from the small body of water.

She started to speak again in the same monotonous voice, quieter this time. "Why is so much of life about pain?"

She turned her head down, and he watched the shiny auburn hair fall and block his view of her face. He wanted to grab it and pull her mouth to his. He resisted. Her question was obviously rhetorical, but he wondered how to respond anyway.

But right then he didn't know either. It had only been a year. One year that he'd known her, and while in some ways it seemed like a long time, in another he couldn't believe he had come to feel like this in such a short period.

It was more than heat. More than how much he loved to be inside her, how she attacked him like the wind that ripped through the trees around them, how he felt like he never wanted to stop fucking her. If he was honest, he'd known it was more than that from the beginning. There was never a pretense that it was "only physical" between them.

But he was also sure neither of them had foreseen what it would grow into. And he had never considered what might happen at the end.

Now he didn't have a choice.

His eyes roved around the land surrounding them. Autumn's richly colored leaves spotted the ground, not yet abundant enough to cover the dull green grass. A haze still hung in the air, though the sun had held court over the clouds for the last several moments. A dense throng of trees surrounded them, and while a few similar clusters dotted the nearby plain, the land was mostly clear as it expanded all the way to the base of the mountains. There it turned upward like the abrupt ascent of a roller coaster.

Her voice resumed once more. "He was such a good cat – first one I ever had."

"I'm sorry," he said, realizing he should have said that when she first mentioned it.

"Not your fault," she answered faintly.

The breeze that flew past was chilly. He felt a brief shiver as he took a deep breath and stood up. The mountains seemed closer to the sky than to them. He remembered when he had first moved to Oregon ten years before how he'd seen the mountains from a distance and automatically registered them as low, still clouds, having never been around mountains before.

He kicked through the sparse leaves toward the pond. Gazing down at the less than healthy-looking grass, he stopped and crushed his hands hard into his jeans pockets. He needed some physical pressure to ground him.

He didn't want her to go. Thinking about it made breathing difficult. Yet here they were. In a matter of minutes he would take her back to her car, and she would go back home to her husband and children, and they would start the drive across the country. She was leaving, and there wasn't anything he could do about it.

A squirrel skittered through the dry leaves several yards in front of him and leapt onto the trunk of a pine tree. It rushed up into the branches out of sight. He breathed in the scent of pine. He'd known the smell for years, but now it made him think only of her. He wondered if it always would.

He thought about all the times in the past year they'd been in these woods together, sitting on the bench where she sat now. He thought of how many times he'd been inside her, both of them mostly clothed in the chilly fall air, her panties pushed out of the way beneath her wool skirt, stockings still in place, his cock freed from his jeans. Or sweating in the mild summer heat, driving into her from behind as she leaned over and clung to the back of the bench, her cutoffs around her ankles. He felt himself start to get hard thinking about it.

It wasn't as though he hadn't known there was a chance of her leaving. In fact, she'd mentioned it when they'd first met, back when he'd had no idea it would ever matter to him. Her husband was being considered for a position in Miami, one that would mean a substantial promotion that he wouldn't turn down. She had told him that she had no intention of leaving her husband. Her children wouldn't understand – they weren't old enough to deal with that kind of thing. She was very committed to her children, even if that meant doing whatever she needed to do to keep her family physically together. He had always admired that about her.

Right now he hated it.

He reached down and picked up the gray pebble he'd nudged with the toe of his boot and threw it into the water. It landed with a hollow splash and disappeared.

After today, she wouldn't be coming back to the park anymore. It would no longer be their main meeting place. And though he had spent much of the last ten years of his life in it, he didn't know now if he could ever come back. There was no escaping that it was permanently changed.

As was he.

The leaves crackled under his feet as he turned to look at her. Her head was still down, her cheek now resting on the stiff dark denim of one knee as she hugged it close to her body. He knew she wouldn't divorce her husband. But he wondered now if she wanted to, if she wanted them to be together. That had never really come up. Hadn't things changed for her? Wasn't this hurting her too? His chest tightened, and he took a deep breath. He didn't know how, after so much time, he could still so often not know what she was feeling. Sometimes he wondered if she knew herself.

It occurred to her as she sat there that she'd been bracing herself for a long time against the pain she'd assumed would come. It was a common method of hers. She anticipated the worst, and she prepared herself for it. Sometimes the worst didn't come. *Usually* the worst didn't come. And sometimes, bad things came that she didn't even think to foresee, for which she didn't have the chance to brace herself. It hadn't occurred to her that spring morning nineteen years ago that her father would leave for work and find her beloved cat on the side of the road near their house. No bracing there. Just searing pain.

She focused on a misshaped pinecone near the edge of the water. She didn't want to leave. Other options weren't viable, and she hadn't been opposed last year when her husband had suggested the possibility of moving to Miami. But that was before. The thought of moving away now filled her with longing and dread.

She wondered if he knew it was almost all because of him. She hadn't told him. Letting him know she was hurting would just make things hurt more. What was the point of that?

And there was no way she could stay here with him. She swallowed. She hadn't mentioned that she had thought about it, of course. That the idea of initiating divorce proceedings was a possibility. But she didn't know how to even begin doing such a thing. The idea was so far outside familiar territory she felt terrified and utterly alone even thinking about it.

Besides, her story was solid. She had told him from the beginning that she wouldn't. It was understood. So bringing it up would just invite vulnerability and uncertainty and make things messy.

The royal blue of his windbreaker filled her peripheral vision. She raised her head to look at him. He was facing away from her, toward the pine trees to her left. As she watched, a squirrel tore across the ground and bounded up into one of them. She stared at the windbreaker's shiny blue fabric and thought about never again seeing it draped across the back of the gray leather chair in her living room – or leaning against it while he bent her over that chair and took her from behind. Never again feeling him inside of her right here on this bench, their breath appearing in the cold winter air as she slid up and down his cock ever so slowly. She used to grin as she saw the urgency in his eyes, wanting her to bounce faster, while she teased him, moving at the slow speed of the frigid water that just barely ruffled behind them in the breeze.

She'd lived in cities most of her life, and the two years she'd spent in inland Oregon were the first time she'd lived away from one. At first she'd hated that. It made her nervous to not be in the middle of a frenzy of strangers with schedules and agendas and appointments, the mutual environment of pressure and rushing allowing thousands of people to pass within inches of each other and not even notice one another. For months, she hadn't even noticed the radiance of the Oregon landscape, much less gone out of her way to seek it out.

He, on the other hand, loved nature. When they'd met, he'd brought her here to the park and talked to her about the wildlife and the vegetation and the ecosystem. In the beginning, they'd sat on the bench and held hands and listened to the silence. She'd look around and marvel at an atmosphere where the city didn't dominate everywhere she looked.

Without consciously noticing it, she'd adjusted to the energy of the natural environment. Now it held an appeal for her that she hadn't even recognized until she thought about leaving it. Last week, on her way to her last day of work, she'd stared out the window and really looked at what she was passing. She drove as the sun came up, not yet visible from behind the towering mountains on her left but seeping its even orange reach indirectly across the sky. On her right a field stretched out like it had never heard of mountains.

It was then she realized the inexplicable sense of peace she felt when she looked around and saw only nature. It was as though its intangible essence leaked in through invisible spaces in her car and enveloped her, undaunted by her lack of conscious attention to its beauty.

And somehow, it had everything to do with him.

They had kissed for the first time on the bench where she now sat. She had turned his direction to look behind them, having heard the brush move and wanting to see what was there. As she did, he reached up to massage her neck, and her breath caught in her throat. She'd sat still, positioned almost touching him and facing behind them, the squirrel that had made the noise munching frantically on an acorn it held between its rigid paws. As his fingers barely moved against her scalp, she had found herself whispering breathlessly in his ear that she didn't remember the last time anything felt so good.

And it was true. After a few seconds, he had answered, his voice as low as the breeze around them.

"I know I might never get to have you." His voice had held the yearning of winter grass buried under the frost. "But," he'd halted, and she'd held her breath. He'd continued in a raw, ragged, whispered voice, one twisted by nervousness and arousal. "I want to kiss you. I want it so badly. I've been thinking about it ever since I knew I was going to see you today."

Her breath had become jagged, his hand still brushing against her hair. She couldn't remember what she'd said in response. But eventually she had noticed the shifting that was taking place, as slow and perhaps as inevitable as the sunrise. Deliberately or not, they were moving closer to facing each other.

She remembered the silence she heard at that moment. Their cheeks had been touching, and he was moving so slowly it was almost imperceptible. For just a moment she found herself thinking, "Oh, god, he might kiss me," in the lightest mental whisper before their mouths were aligned, and there was no time to catch her breath before they slid together. There had been no space left between them.

Now, he stood facing away from her, toward the water off which she'd heard the insects ricocheting so many times the next summer as she rode him with abandon on the hard bench beneath her, crying out for all the wildlife and vegetation and ecosystem to hear. There weren't that many places they had appeared together in public. Aside from their respective residences, most of their rendezvous had occurred right where she sat. A bench she would most likely never see again, in a park where she would most likely never again be.

In a few days she would be living in Miami. She wouldn't drive anymore past the park's big wooden sign that hung with tiny glittering icicles in the winter and commanded a bright circular flower bed in the summer, knowing she would be seeing him in a matter of moments. The vivid purple and yellow and fuchsia blooms would be thousands of miles away from her when summer next came. She would be back in the city again. And he wouldn't be there to take her away, out into the realm of the earth and living things that weren't people. He wouldn't be there at all.

She met the hard stare of the gray horizon and studied the uneven line of mountaintops for what would likely be the last time. It was time to go.

He studied the water in front of him, the feeling that she was about to walk out of his life lodged in the pit of his stomach. He thought of her comment about why life was so full of pain. He didn't know, but he knew he was at its mercy now. And he had no idea when it would stop.

Would she miss him?

Gray twilight crept in around them. He lifted his eyes and noticed that the clouds had overcome the sun and now blanketed all he could see with a neutral bleakness. The mountains in the distance meshed with the sky, reminding him of the way they'd looked that first time he'd ever laid eyes on the horizon in his new home in eastern Oregon. He pushed his hands back into his pockets and turned around. Back toward her. As he did, she looked up and met his eyes. She looked away quickly as she spoke.

"I was just thinking it's about time to go." Her voice sounded tight.

He studied her. "No."

She looked up at him with surprise. She started to speak again, but he was already striding toward her, pulling her unceremoniously from the bench and up against him, kissing her with the solidity of the mountains behind him, which he pictured watching with approval.

She didn't need convincing. Her body responded to him the way it always had, and soon she was clawing at his jacket, at everything that separated her from him, and he was shrugging out of it and pushing hers from her shoulders, their eyes closed, nothing but harsh, frantic kissing between them as he ripped her blouse open and she tore off his belt.

Their clothes all came off this time, landing in a stack beside them. They ignored the bench as he all but threw her to the ground. She barely noticed the rough pine needles under her skin as she heard him rip open a condom, still kissing her. Then she felt him inside her, and a sob almost broke her veneer. She fought to breathe, feeling the burn in her core, pushing against him to turn them over so she could sit straight on top, riding his cock as if propelled by the very force of the earth itself.

He reached up and grabbed her hair, pulling her head down to his.

"I want you to stay," he hissed in her ear, and the veneer shattered. Her breath turned to a sob, and she fell against him, pushing herself onto him in rhythm with her crying. He turned them back over and drove into her, fiercely, as if he could force things through the power of their fucking to be the way he wanted them to. Harder and harder he fucked her, her wails sounding animalistic in the primal woods. The birds murmured around them, in sympathy he liked to think.

Her cheeks were streaked with tears. He felt even as she clung to him that something was breaking inside her, and he held her hair tighter to let her know he was there. He was there. He would break with her if he had to.

"I want you, I want you, I want you," he whispered harshly in her ear, the words shooting forth like the throbbing of his cock, well within his possession but beyond his control.

She cried, pulling his body into hers, eyes closed, her face a scrunched-up picture of potency and immediacy. It was when he looked at it that he felt something break in himself.

"I want you too," she whispered, her eyes still closed.

He buried his face in her shoulder, feeling her tears against his ear as he pushed into her. She wrapped her legs around him so tightly it almost hurt, her hands gripping the back of his neck. Suddenly her sobbing intensified, and he knew she was coming, though she rarely had in that position. Her body writhed wildly beneath him, her voice raw. Her breath was ragged as she finished, catching periodically as her body shuddered.

He kissed her and then came inside her, gripping her hair as his climax unleashed the ferocity inside him, the desperate frustration and carnality and longing that had driven him since he pulled her from the bench.

He could barely bring himself to pull out of her as he slid off her body, dropping his head to the ground as they came together side by side on their backs. She touched her head to his shoulder.

The sun was back, streaking through the cloud cover to hit the tops of the pine trees like fire. She could see the individual needles, brandished by the light, glowing like the sun was shooting through just for them.

"Like gold-plated pine needles," she whispered, barely aware she had spoken out loud. Glittering above them, they sparkled like the sun itself for another few seconds before an unseen cloud slid in, fading them back to deep matte green.

He made a small noise, acknowledging the change. "You know what they say," he murmured after a moment. His eyes closed. "All that glitters...." She heard the quiet sadness in his voice as he left her to fill in the rest.

She repeated the saying in her mind and looked up at the pine needles again, rich and smooth and green far above them. To her, they still glittered. Her gaze dropped to the ring on her left hand. She didn't know what made gold such a high standard.

To Make It That Way

When people tell me I seem different now, my stomach clenches for a moment. At those times, there are two things I know: one, that they're right, and two, that even though I am aware of why, I could never explain exactly what happened to make it that way. It was, and still is, an enigma in my life.

I was twenty-one when I met her. Three of my friends and I were standing outside one of the bars we went to all the time when she pulled up in her black Toyota sedan. I glanced over, and her eyes fastened on mine with an expression I couldn't begin to decipher. It was an expression I would come to know well. It meant that she was seeing me, really seeing me, and that she saw something I needed that she knew she could give me.

"You," she said to me. Her voice was sweet but had an edge of command that made me jump even as she smiled. I moved forward to her open passenger-side window and looked in at her.

She nodded at the bar. "You going in there to get laid, sweetheart?" I just stared at her, at a loss for what to say. Behind me, I could hear my tipsy friends shuffling and murmuring.

Her smile grew wider. "Why don't you come with me instead." She kept her eyes on mine, and I grew no less stupefied as the seconds ticked by. I thought I hadn't understood her correctly and didn't give the idea that she was serious more than a second's – though an elated second's – thought. Then she lowered her voice and made her intentions perfectly clear.

That's when I got nervous. I wasn't into casual sex – had never had it, actually – and sex in general, much as I craved it, made me shrink back in fear that I wasn't doing something (anything) right. My shyness had kept me from having it as much as I could have, and I had only slept with two women. One was my girlfriend right after we graduated high school, and we waited so long that my performance anxiety was camouflaged among the closeness we had developed. The other was a girl I had dated about a year before for a few months, and I attributed the fact that our sex had never been fantastic to my own inadequacy.

Now a woman whose expertise I could only imagine sat in front of me, already fucking me with her eyes and expressing unambiguous interest in me. Petrified, I said the first thing that came into my mind:

"Um, don't you think we should go out or something first?"

She laughed out loud, a spontaneous, hearty laugh that I knew was not mocking me. She shifted into park, smiled at my friends over my shoulder and called to them.

"Do you guys mind if I borrow your friend for a while? I'll see that he gets home safe and sound," she said with a wink after they'd bumbled forward to crowd around the window. When my buddy Jake finally came to his senses and made some reply, Cole, whose name I didn't yet know, placed her graceful hand on the gearshift and nodded. "Hop in, darling."

I did, and she shifted back into drive and took me to her house.

Thus began what seemed like a sudden double life for me. I still hung out with my friends on weekends and most other times we usually had. But sometimes I disappeared for a while. I often lost track of time when Cole summoned me – or, considerably less often, when I called upon her – to get together for one of our fervent, marathon, phenomenal sex sessions that left me feeling like the rest of the world had evaporated or that we'd stepped onto another timeless planet for a while. Not many people even knew about her, and those that did didn't hear much about her. She slipped in and out of my life like an intoxicating scent – not there for long, but hitting with such force that it left an impression time has its work cut out to erase.

She lived by herself. No pets, no plants, no evidence of any live entities to which she was responsible other than herself. I hardly said a word as she drove us from the bar to her house that night, and she let me sit in silence, a quiet, serene smile on her face as her wrist rested casually on the top of the steering wheel, her eyes settled on the road in front of us.

After she led me inside, she threw her jacket over the back of a dining room chair and turned and offered me her hand. "Nicolette," she said simply, her lips opening in a smile. "You can call me Cole."

Her smile seemed to be knowing, sly, rather Cheshire Cat-ish, and I couldn't imagine of what secret she was in possession. She was gorgeous: striking peach complexion, tall graceful figure, blonde hair cut in a way that seemed to invite pieces of it to fall sexily in front of one eye. I had wondered then how old she was. I didn't know yet that she was 40 – and I never would have from her appearance.

"I'm Zack," I said, immediately disgusted by how weak my voice sounded. But her smile didn't waver. I glanced around me. In the bathroom down the hall I saw a corset and several pairs of stockings hanging from the shower rod.

She saw me looking. "I collect lingerie," she explained, moving in front of me to the kitchen.

"Lingerie. That's interesting."

She smiled. "I'm glad you think so. Some of it requires hand washing, which is why it's in there. Would you like some tea?"

Tea. It didn't seem to fit the occasion. She reached into a cupboard toward a high shelf and glanced back at me. Her thin sweater slipped a bit over her shoulder and displayed a slender black strap.

I nodded and moved back into the dining room, suddenly so nervous I didn't even want to be around her. Much as this situation could lead to something I certainly wanted, I was so scared right then that I just wanted to be somewhere else. I would have preferred by multitudes to be home in my boxers playing video games.

I heard her shriek and stepped back into the kitchen.

"Shit," she said, looking down at her top. Water had bounced off the side of the tea kettle and splattered all over the front of her. I stared at the dark wet splotches, almost covering her breasts and splaying up to her neck.

Christ.

"I'm going to have to change," she said, smiling at me as she headed toward the stairs. As she ascended them I caught a glimpse of her sweater being pulled over her head and the shiny black and lace underneath it.

If I'd been a little more sure of myself, I would have followed her up to the bedroom and ripped off the rest of her clothes. Even despite my nervousness, that urge was uppermost on my mind. With a deep breath I turned toward the kitchen door just as she reentered through it. As we almost collided, she gave me a glittering smile and moved past me to attend to the kettle.

I tried to catch my breath.

She'd put on a black oversize button-down shirt. The top two buttons were undone, and when she turned to take the kettle off the stove, the collar slid to the edge of her shoulder. There was no strap this time.

That's when I felt myself get hard. I wanted to walk up behind her and rip her shirt the rest of the way off, grab her tits and –

"Sugar?" her voice cut into my fantasy.

"Huh? Sugar. Yes." Maddeningly, I blushed as I looked down. It was funny how I could clearly imagine what I wanted to do to her, but standing right there with the opportunity to, I was scared shitless to try.

Suddenly I noticed her little smile as she watched the white grains slide into the steaming liquid. Something that had been vaguely swirling in my head solidified: she knew precisely the effect she was having on me.

My eyes narrowed. Did she enjoy the way this was tormenting me?

"Cream?" She turned what appeared to be innocent blue eyes to me again. I looked back at her, and the urge to kiss her became overwhelming.

"Yes," I said, and moved forward before I could stop myself. I pressed my mouth to hers and felt her tongue slide against mine. I pushed her back against the counter and wrapped my arms around her waist.

That was the end of what I initiated. She took over from there, dropping us both to the kitchen floor and straddling me as she pulled her still-buttoned shirt over her head. She was naked underneath, and the memory of that first glorious view of her full, round tits and the way she ran her fingertips over her nipples can still make me hard. She had a condom in her jeans pocket, and she fucked me right there on the kitchen floor before any nervousness in me had time to catch up.

As she later told me was her objective, I was never scared to make a move with her again.

Much as Cole was obviously in charge of our sexual encounters – and just about everything else, it seemed – she loved to be dominated, and she was teaching me things I'd never dreamed of about rough sex.

"Pull my hair," she said once as we stood in her living room, her blue eyes trained on mine. I noticed again the effortless sweetness in her voice even amidst the edge of command.

I reached up and clasped a handful, giving it a hesitant tug.

"Pull it," she said as she reached up and gripped my forearm, snapping it back once with a speed and brevity that surprised me.

I swallowed. I pulled again with the same sharp, no-nonsense force I had felt her use.

Her eyes glimmered. "Better. How do you like that?"

She looked at me steadily. I wasn't sure what the right answer was.

Knowing my thoughts in a way that had become so common it was hardly surprising anymore, she said, "I'm not looking for a 'right' answer, Zack. I'm looking for *your* answer."

I wasn't sure what that was either.

"I like it because you like it," I said finally.

She nodded, eyes locked on mine.

"And I like it because... I don't know why," I faltered.

"Did it make you uncomfortable?" she asked, and somehow I knew despite her neutral countenance that if I said yes, she would never ask me to do it again.

But it hadn't. I mean, it had, but it hadn't because she liked it. I wouldn't have dreamed of doing it on my own. I told her as much.

"Appropriate." She gave another nod. "It's not something you should do if you don't know someone likes it. There are a lot of things like that. Many of them you'll be doing with me. How do you feel about spanking?"

"What?" I immediately blushed at such a stupid answer. It wasn't like I hadn't watched porn. I knew some people were into spanking. I just hadn't done it.

"I don't know," I said. "It seems... violent or something. Or degrading." Yet somehow I knew it wasn't, knew it was different. But I wasn't sure how, and some part of me seemed unable to reconcile it with that conception.

Cole's eyes glinted. "Sex," she said, "has the potential to encompass and represent all human experience. All the nuances, all the understood and not understood, may be experienced through sex. And that means there's a whole realm of it we're not going to understand. It's beyond our common forms of understanding." Her eyes bore into me like steel. "But it's not beyond our experiencing."

After a moment she broke her gaze, and I noticed I started breathing again. I also noticed my cock was rock-hard.

"The key," she said, lifting her water glass from the end table near where we stood, "is in awareness, respect, openness, authenticity. We don't have to understand it all, as long as we're aware of ourselves. As long as we respect our partners. As long as we approach with openness what is happening between us. And as long as we are authentic in our dealings, our experiences, our examinations. If something is uncomfortable, examine that and see what it teaches you. If it feels inauthentic, stop doing it. "

"That wouldn't account for a lot of abusive situations where sex is concerned," I countered. "Lots of people may think they're aware of and like what they're doing, but it hurts someone else or is even criminal."

"Yes," she agreed, setting her water glass back down. "But that means at least one of those pieces is missing."

I pondered that, as she didn't appear inclined to expound. She moved toward me and caught my mouth with hers, and I caught my breath at the suddenness, at the heat that zipped through me like lightning at her touch. She backed me up against the couch until I fell onto it, my hands groping her breasts. Pulling my cock out of my jeans, Cole dropped her head and sucked with fervor, going after my cock like she was possessed, as though she was taking something from it she needed.

With a final pump, she paused, running her tongue up the length of my shaft. Her cat-like eyes gazed up at me, hard lust and a hint of something else glowing in them. Abruptly she stood up on the couch, towering over me as she pulled off her shirt and stepped out of her jeans. Underneath them she wore an impeccable red lingerie set, glimmering bra, thong, and garter belt with rhinestones embedded around the rims and matching stockings. I caught my breath.

Cole didn't need lingerie, but she sure knew how to use it.

I was still tingling from the cocksucking she'd just given me, feeling practically euphoric but awaiting instructions. I watched her, not knowing what she was going to demand of me.

She threw her jeans aside and stood above me on the couch, one foot planted on either side of my thighs. Her gaze rested on mine as each garter was individually undone and the garter belt, thong, and bra slid off one by one. I broke eye contact to look at her naked pussy above me, then quickly flicked my eyes back to hers.

"What do you want, Zack?" she broke the silence with.

What did I want? What did she mean? The question was a departure from the order I had been anticipating, and I didn't know how to address it.

I saw the smile in her cobalt eyes before it reflected in the curve of her lips. It was that same smile, the one I'd seen when she'd pulled up in her car outside the bar that night, the one she'd given me when she first told me her name, the one she'd flashed as she'd gone up to the bedroom to change out of her wet sweater. The one I never determined what lay behind, that was always the same for her but seemed to bring such a wild variety of things out of me. The one that, to this day, may still be the strongest visual memory I have of her.

"What do you want, Zack," she repeated, a statement this time. "Why are you waiting for me to tell you what to do? Do you think that's your job? Be told what to do and do it? What do *you* want?"

I swallowed. To be told what to do *was* what I wanted. How else would I know?

Cole continued to stand above me, her naked pussy shimmering. "Yes, I know you feel like you don't want that responsibility." The smile was still in place. In a lithe movement she sank down onto me, straddling my body but not taking me inside her. She leaned forward.

"But you have it anyway."

I looked at her tits, naked and easily within reach in front of me. I wanted to grab them.

She was watching me. She ran her own hands lightly over her breasts, a lock of blonde hair falling in front of one cat eye. "I'm not always going to be here to tell you what to do, Zack. Trust yourself. What you want is just as important as what anyone else wants." She looked at me. "Do you understand?"

I grabbed at her, shoving her hands out of the way and squeezing her tits, sitting up a little to yank her down on top of me. Indignation and embarrassment rose in me as I felt uncertain, wanting to show her for once that I knew something she didn't. I wanted to show her I could know what to do, that I could do something on my own.

I reached up and grabbed her hair, and she expelled a hot breath as I yanked it back and turned us over, pushing my body on top of hers. I reached for a condom from the pile on the end table and tore it open. When it was on, I grasped at her throat, administering a firm chokehold like she'd shown me how to do not long before. I met her eyes as I reached for her dripping pussy, molten liquid covering my fingers like the heat from her eyes covered my entire body. I circled her clit like she'd taught me until she came, my body trembling almost as much as hers when I finally pulled my hand away.

I pushed my cock into her and pounded, feeling the same way Cole had looked when she'd sucked my cock moments before – like I was possessed, needing something that was inside her as I drilled into her and she screamed my name, clawing at the cushions around us. I yelled as I came, something I'd never done before, and collapsed on top of her, panting.

She panted too beneath me. As our breathing slowed, gently she reached and touched my cheek. The unexpected tenderness gave me pause. I lifted my head and met her gaze.

Only once did we run into each other unexpectedly in public. Some friends and I had decided to stop at a coffee shop near her neighborhood on the way home from a concert. I saw her as soon as we walked in. Momentarily paralyzed, I didn't know what to do. For some reason I felt uncomfortable mixing the two sides of my life – the Cole side and the non-Cole side. It was like they represented two different selves for me, and I didn't yet know how to put them together.

Concentrating on a notebook on the table in front of her, she didn't see me as we ordered and sat at a booth on the opposite side of the cafe. Jake finally noticed my distracted state and, when he followed my eyes, recognized Nicolette immediately. Since two of the guys we were with hadn't been there the night I'd met her, Jake enthusiastically filled them in while I sat in conspicuous silence. Suddenly everyone at the table was pushing, wondering why I wasn't going over to see her. Comments about how hot she was intermingled with pointed urges for me to approach her. Finally I knew I'd rather go talk to her than listen to their shit for another second.

She looked up at the sound of her name; I stood in front of her. She smiled slowly, and suddenly I knew she had known I was there. She looked me up and down before re-meeting my eyes.

"Hello," she said pleasantly, motioning toward the chair across from her. I sat. I tried not to fidget nervously, but I knew I failed.

"Here by yourself?" she asked. Her eyes sparkled. She knew I wasn't.

I considered lying to her but decided I would be neither convincing nor comfortable with that. So I shook my head and said what I hoped was casually, "Nah, I'm with some friends." I indicated them with a jerk of my head.

She nodded, that maddeningly knowing smile on her face.

"Hmmm." She tipped her chair back and smiled wider. She was about to embark on some spiel, I could tell. Just once I wanted to tell her I already knew what she told me, or thought it was wrong and could give a good reason why, or that I'd already tried it and it didn't work. Each time, in fact, I braced myself to give her one of these very responses, but each time she managed to convey things in a way that was so obvious that I couldn't try to dispel it without looking stupid. I was never good with bullshit anyway. Then I would end up mad and glaring at her, at that knowing smile, small and subtle as if it existed just for me, and just want to smack her, and soon we would be wrapped together naked, sweating and squeezing and screaming...

"Let me guess." Her voice interrupted my thoughts just before my cock got hard. My thoughts veered from the hot to the dull as I focused my attention on her smooth monologue. "Your friends saw me and recognized me. You're in one of your serious moods, and possibly due to some ambivalent feelings of which I'm unaware, you felt uncomfortable encountering me in public when you were with your friends, whom you probably haven't told much about me." She winked as I glowered at her. "But they teased you and made you feel stupid for passing up the chance to come over here when it meant you'd get laid – so you came over even though you didn't really want to."

I don't know how the fuck she knew everything. I hated that my behavior was so easy to predict; I didn't know if it signified a weakness of mine or a strength of hers.

"Why would you think that?" I thought my voice sounded decently defiant, and I was proud of myself.

Cole glanced down at the drink she was holding and chuckled. "I have supreme confidence, Zack, that someday you'll learn not to let other people dictate your actions like that," she said as she looked back up.

I glared at her, and when she smiled again, I got pissed at the same time a jolt of arousal shot through me. I clenched my jaw and tried to look away, but my eyes locked on a blonde wisp of her hair that fell across her cheekbone. I wanted her. Now.

She held my gaze. In the span of a few seconds, all but the active desire to fuck her became distant priorities in my consciousness. My cock strained against the zipper of my jeans, and I wanted her to yank it out and take it in her mouth right there.

Cole stood and swung her purse over her shoulder. She must have packed up her things sometime during our conversation when I wasn't paying attention. She looked down at me.

"Let's go."

I stood up and followed her without so much as a glance back at my friends. She led me to her car in the back of the dark parking lot and opened the back door, nodding for me to get in. After I did, she climbed in after me and shut the door, reaching up front for the lock button.

When she turned back to me she immediately grabbed my zipper and yanked it down. In seconds my cock was out in the cold night air, and her gaze rested on mine for a second before she dropped her head and took the length of it to the back of her throat. I groaned and grabbed her hair. She started sucking hard and fast, and I was going to come if she didn't stop soon. I pulled her hair gently, and she rose off me as I throbbed with the urge to explode.

I looked at her, breathing heavily, and she pulled a condom from her pocket. She seemed to carry them wherever she went. She watched me as she unrolled it slowly down my cock. Then she sat back on her heels for a moment and looked at me. Even in the dark I could see that smile lurking in her features. It was almost as though I could sense it by now.

Just as I was about to say something, she moved forward, and I thought I heard a low chuckle just before she straddled me, hiking up her skirt and pulling her thong off to the side. I reached up and pulled her down on top of me, pushing my hands under her shirt to her flesh. She rode me hard, moaning into my neck as I slid my hands under her bra. Then she sat back up, blonde locks swishing around her face as she bounced on top of me and I closed my eyes, knowing I was going to come if I looked at her. I heard her gasp, and when I opened my eyes she was working her fingers over her clit, getting herself off. I grabbed her thighs as I came too, shuddering as she bucked and squeezed around me.

Cole climbed off me and reached under her skirt to reposition her thong as I grabbed a tissue from the box she conveniently kept tossed around her vehicle and took the condom off. She reached behind her for the door handle, and in seconds we were standing back in the parking lot again.

She chuckled. "Thanks, Zack. Go on back to your friends." That beautiful smile was back on her face as she gave me a long kiss. With a wink, she opened the car door and climbed in, leaving my thoughts to pick up where they had left off back inside at her table.

I learned a lot from Cole. Some of it I think I haven't even realized yet. And though I haven't seen her in almost a year, I still think about her. Once in a while my friends still mention "that hot older lady you slept with for a while." But they don't understand. What they do know about it is merely the surface, nothing of what was underneath, where the two of us were – and where no one else could see. I have no idea where she is now, but every time I stand outside that bar or find myself in the parking lot of that cafe, I remember that indescribable smile and how, for a time, she directed it at me. It's hard to say whether that omniscience she exuded in my eyes was really there or whether it was the youth and naiveté in me that displayed it, in reflection, only to me. I still can't convince myself that Nicolette wasn't something special, someone with that intangible ability to see inside people and know what they need. Maybe she thought I didn't need her anymore. My emotional investment made it impossible to see if that was true. It seems to me everyone needs her.

Sometimes I wonder what I meant to her life. It's hard to imagine I had anywhere near the impact on her that she had on me, but I suppose it's impossible to say. It's just another one of the mysteries that, as intimately as I knew her in some ways, I will never know about Cole. By now I don't yearn for her anymore, and it isn't even that painful, which was once hard for me to imagine. I still hold out hope that someday I'll get to see her again. I've finally come to accept what somewhere inside me I've always known: if she wants it to happen, it will.

On the Rise

Sheila lowered her mouth slowly, sliding her lips over his erection with the care of a seasoned artisan. She was surprised to feel herself savoring the experience; the sensation in her core was more than concern for how he was feeling, how he was finding the blowjob she had just commenced. It was arousal. Strong arousal. It increased when the tip of his cock nestled against the back of her throat and she heard his sharp intake of breath. She paused for a second, relishing the feeling of fullness in her mouth, before pulling back slowly. She pulled her lips all the way off his sheathed cock, flicking her tongue out to lap at the end as she backed up and looked up at him.

He was breathing heavily, staring down at her like she was the star that lit the very moon as the cock in front of her bobbed slightly, as though to wave her attention back to it. All the hesitation, embarrassment, dejectedness was gone from his eyes. The only things in them now were lust, desire, craving of the satisfaction of this single moment as though it was all that had ever mattered in the world.

Sheila's stomach jumped at the sight, and she felt her pussy moisten. Holding his gaze, she inched her face back toward his cock, extending her tongue as she neared him. Allen's head dropped head back, a groan emitting from his throat as she made contact with the condom that covered him, sealing her lips around the head of his cock and sighing as she pushed her head almost to the base of his shaft. His hands gripped the arms of his chair, and she could sense him wanting to grab her head and shove it down hard until the hot come she imagined was waiting just under the surface exploded against her throat.

She smiled as best she could as she drew back up, preparing to give him permission to do just that.

A week earlier Sheila had stared at her computer screen, her frown pronounced. Eventually, without her noticing, her expression softened into a wistful grimace as her eyes shifted from the screen to the window by her desk.

It wasn't the first time she'd read the article. It wasn't even the second. Since she'd encountered it a month before, she'd returned to the bookmarked page and read the words there time and again, even as it so wrenched the place where basic human empathy resided in her to do so.

She twirled her chair and prepared to get up. Then she stopped, falling back against the back and faltering, for nowhere near the first time, in the midst of returning to her normal routine after reading the searing account she just had.

She'd stopped so many times because she wondered what to do. Whether she could help, how she could help if so, and if doing what little she had the opportunity to would even matter in the end. Each time, she had contemplated a little longer and eventually gotten up with a sad sigh and within a little while had forgotten about the article she'd first read after the link caught her eye the month before.

Until the next time she recalled and returned to it.

Her business phone buzzed, indicating a text message. She went to it and registered the name of one of her regulars sending a polite greeting and a request for an appointment. She checked her calendar and replied in the affirmative for the date he had proposed. Then she entered it in her schedule and went back to her chair.

The article was still open on the screen in front of her. *"In the last decade, the number of nursing home residents as young as in their twenties has been gradually on the rise."* Her eyes slid over the words she'd read numerous times, then moved to the picture accompanying the article of the 27-year-old former firefighter whose first quote appeared in the next paragraph. He'd been knocked from a ladder by a backdraft during a fire rescue, and both his legs were paralyzed now. He lived in an assisted-living home.

Sheila's eyes narrowed in sympathy as she read of the juxtaposition of living amongst the elderly residents in the facility in the small city where he lived. Words and phrases jumped out at her, ones that had particularly caught her eye the first time she'd read the story. "Lonely"... "isolated" ... "no privacy." The piece went on to explain that in some retirement homes, younger people were housed together, and targeted activities were planned for them. But where this young man was, he was by far the youngest resident, and the numbers were too small for that to be relevant.

Allen Leichter. She'd remembered his name since she'd first read it in the caption. His words were on the page beside it. *"You just sit here, day after day, not knowing if this is where you're going to spend the rest of your life."*

She had yet to read the article without crying.

Brian had obviously perused her website thoroughly when he contacted her. Her website was far more than a simple advertisement; rather, it was a detailed account of her perspectives, attunements, and proclivities, as well as a summary of what she felt she could offer prospective clients. It was clear when he contacted her that Brian had read it top to bottom, going so far as to quote things straight from the page when he detailed his proposal. She wondered how many others he had read about, how much time he had spent researching what he was looking for.

Brian was quoted in the article about young people in retirement homes. He was Allen Leichter's best friend; the article said Brian came to visit him most days. The existence of a friend like that made Sheila tear up with gratitude for the beauty in humanity.

Sheila wasn't sure why it had taken Brian so long to contact her or someone like her. Allen had been injured almost a year ago. She wondered if, even seeing him in person most days, Brian hadn't really understood the things Allen shared with the reporter who wrote about him and others like him living in an environment of confinement, loneliness, muted desolation. Brian went off and about his life each day after he left Allen. Perhaps seeing it in black and white brought him closer to understanding what his friend experienced in the meantime.

Or perhaps it was something else. Sheila didn't know, of course, but all that really mattered was that Brian had contacted her now. He had made an offer, or more like a request, really, and she had accepted his invitation to consider it and get back to him.

She didn't know why she hesitated, exactly. She had a high level of confidence in her professional capabilities. Back when she first began escorting and was working full-time, she had serviced many clients of differing ages, circumstances, and temperaments. That was part of the job.

Sheila only worked as an escort part-time now. She had sustained enough regulars and earned enough per appointment that she didn't need to work more than that to support herself. In fact, she rarely engaged new clients anymore. The handful of regulars with whom she had familiar professional relationships was generally all she needed to maintain her income. It was virtually ideal, and it had been a long time coming. She had worked hard to build those relationships, and she appreciated its paying off, both literally and figuratively.

Escorting wasn't a throwaway job for her. She was well aware that the level at which she worked required a specific skill set, one that not everyone had and that she had worked to cultivate. Yes, some of it she'd had inclinations toward at the outset, but the capacities always had room to be refined. Sensitivity. Appreciation. Awareness. Listening.

Fucking was, by a long shot, not all she did for a living.

Brian had seemed to know that – or pick it up somehow by reading her website. But she had never specialized in disability. In this case, she acknowledged, it wasn't the disability itself that struck her so much. It was the environment, the tragic wretchedness of what Allen's life was now, the searing loss of freedom of which his environment had to constantly remind him. Could she enter that kind of desolation and have anything to offer in the face of it?

She wondered if Brian was pursuing other escorts in the meantime. His budget was limited, he'd said, and there was a likelihood any meeting with Allen would be a one-time occurrence. Something about that made Sheila cringe even more at the idea. Would there be any value, anything redeeming, in being handed an experience a single time that would likely never be repeated, that might do little more than remind one of what one used to have access to freely? She didn't know.

When she'd shared that with Brian, he'd said, "That's one of the reasons I contacted you. Because you care. You may not know, and to tell you the truth, I don't either. But it occurred to you to care. I think being exposed to that, however briefly, is something Allen needs. He needs to know somebody cares. Somebody besides me, I mean. Somebody – " he hesitated, and she almost filled in the sentence for him, sensing his hesitation and knowing where he was going. "Somebody female," he finally finished. She could almost hear him blushing.

It was that argument that finally convinced her. Caring couldn't possibly be a drawback, she felt, and in fact, whatever else happened, it could only work in her favor – and, more importantly, his. She pulled up her schedule, quoted her rate for different times, and she and Brian had confirmed an appointment between her and Allen the third time they'd talked on the phone.

Backing away from him, Sheila reached for the top button of her blouse. She had lost track of time; she didn't care how long this appointment lasted. The visitation room was reserved for two hours. Right then, she was content to stay there until they kicked her out.

She pulled open the first button. Watching Allen's eyes glued unabashedly to her chest, she let go of the fabric and brushed her hands over her breasts, letting her fingers slide on down the cool satin to her belly. Gathering the fabric in loose fists, she slid her hands back up, pausing just below the purple lace of her push-up bra. Allen's mouth was slightly open, and his hand went to his cock as she arched her back, sliding the bunched fabric up an inch or two as she bit her lip. She wasn't faking it; there was no question she was turned on by the man who sat in front of her, watching avidly from his motorized wheelchair.

She knew this wasn't new to him. It was obvious from his handsomeness, his age, the experience she could see in his eyes as he in took her performance. He had done all this before.

But not for almost a year. And she tried not to think about how long it might be before it happened again after she left there that day.

It had been years since she'd set foot in a retirement home. Her grandparents had all died more than a decade before; visiting her grandfather just prior to his death had been the last direct experience she'd had with an assisted-living facility.

Allen was better-looking than in the picture that had accompanied the article. Sheila swallowed, uncomfortable for some reason that that had occurred to her. Still, there was a dullness in his brown eyes she had a feeling hadn't always been there. She stepped forward, feeling unusually unsure of herself, and introduced herself. Allen lifted his hand from the arm of his wheelchair to shake hers, replacing it after he let go.

He nodded at the love seat against the wall several feet away, and Sheila moved to it and sat. He didn't make eye contact with her as she looked back at him, smoothing her skirt over her thighs.

"Do you want to come over here a little closer?" Her voice was soft, nonthreatening, the tone intuitively taking on what would be best received under the circumstances. This was a propensity she naturally seemed to have, and it had served her well in her work. More than once she had been complimented on the quality of her voice – not just the words themselves, but her ability to know exactly how to speak and when.

Allen glanced her way, then pushed the motorized button on his chair. It moved forward jerkily, his finger tapping the button a few times until his feet were only several inches from hers. He backed it up and turned a bit so his chair was positioned perpendicular to the love seat.

Abruptly he looked up. His smile seemed hard for him to formulate, but it appeared nonetheless. "Look, I'm – I just want to say I appreciate your coming here." His face burned, and he looked back down. "I don't really know – I don't know really – "

"What to do." Sheila's tone hadn't changed. She saw no need for him to remain in his obvious state of embarrassment and distress when she understood what he was wanting to say.

He let out a breath, then looked up at her. "Yeah. But I didn't want you to think I don't want you here. Or anything like that."

She placed her hand on his arm. He looked down at it and swallowed. "You don't have to know, Allen. You don't have to worry about anything. That's my job." She smiled into his eyes. She considered her next words carefully, wanting to make sure they were true before she allowed herself to speak them.

"And I'm glad to be here."

Brian had said she'd check in at the counter just inside the door of the facility, and a staff member would tell her where to go. Allen had a private room reserved for them. She just had to tell them whom she was there to see.

"Is he able – I mean, can he – " Uncharacteristically, Sheila stumbled over her words, not sure how to ask if she would be pleasuring someone who no longer had erections.

Brian cut her off, to her relief. "Yes. It was mostly nerve damage in his legs rather than an actual spinal cord injury." He'd paused. "He knows I'm... he knows I'm paying you," he added.

Sheila nodded, aware that it would be only practical for Allen to understand that. Part of her job would be to make him forget it.

She reached back for the clasp of her bra, catching her breath as she let the straps fall down her shoulders. She had always been exhibitionistic. Turing someone on who was watching her was one of her biggest aphrodisiacs. This time something about the usual effect was intensified, though everything had seemed to be from the moment she'd walked into the room Allen had reserved. She didn't know why – and it hadn't taken long for her to stop caring, to be caught up enough in what she was doing that such analysis didn't matter.

She unhooked the purple bra and let it drop, taking a deep breath and feeling her chest rise perceptibly as she watched Allen watch her. His eyelids drooped, the view of her tits, naked in front of him, having an effect she couldn't know but took immense enjoyment in imagining. Just out of his reach, she covered them with her hands and squeezed lightly, feeling the heat intensify in her pussy. She inched closer to him and leaned forward, dropping to her hands and knees.

"Do you want to touch them?" she whispered.

For the first time, she got an inkling that Allen might have been sexually dominant before his accident. The clench of his jaw, the forward thrust of energy she felt from his core made her think that if he were capable, he would have leapt at her and held her down on the floor, crushing her under his strong body as he pushed his cock into her and thrust without restraint.

With that image in mind, she adopted his past role and let him live vicariously, practically leaping at him as she clawed her way onto his chair, lifting a knee to rest on one arm of it while she shoved her tits in his face, breathless with the anticipation of feeling his mouth close over them, his teeth against her nipples as he sucked them like a popsicle in the sweltering blanket of August heat.

He didn't disappoint her. His arms rose up as he grasped each breast firmly, yanking one into his mouth and working his tongue over it with a skill she allowed herself to melt into, cooing as he worked back and forth from one to the other until she longed to have his cock deep inside her and pumping with abandon.

That wasn't going to happen today. She gathered a modicum of composure as she gripped the back of his head one more time and then pulled away, dropping to her knees in front of him as she pulled out the condom tucked into the lace top of her stocking and ripped it open, slipping it into her mouth and watching him as she lowered her mouth over his cock, pushing the rubber down with her lips until it covered the hard length pressed against her tongue.

"What kinds of things does he like? What is he interested in? Or what was he, before..." Sheila looked down her mug, not wanting to finish the sentence. Allen's circumstances struck her as so horrific she could hardly stand to think about them. She wondered if that was why she'd really hesitated to take on this client – f it wasn't about him, and worrying whether or not it would really help him to see her, but rather because she couldn't – or didn't want to – handle the discomfort with which the entire situation put her literally face-to-face.

It wasn't a thought she liked. She looked away from her latte and out the window of the coffee shop where she'd met with Brian prior to her appointment with Allen.

"He's into football, movies, actually likes a little bit of poetry. Went to school for astronomy." Brian cleared his throat. "He also liked his job a lot. He was very dedicated to it. He'd been wanting to be a firefighter since we were teenagers. I think if – " He stopped, and when Sheila looked back at him, his gaze was trained the same direction hers had been a moment before. "I mean. I just think, if something like this had to happen... he'd prefer it to have happened as a result of doing his job.

"He saved someone's life, you know."

Sheila stared at him. She hadn't known. The article hadn't mentioned it.

As though guessing what she was thinking, Brian met her eyes and said, "He doesn't talk about it much. It's not the kind of thing he would take credit for. He feels like it would look like he was just trying to color the way people saw him now, in his condition. Or something."

It probably would, Sheila thought. She waited for Brian to continue.

"But he did. He was climbing the ladder to the third floor to get a 16-year-old kid who lived in the building out. His parents had told Allen the kid was still in there."

Brian looked down at the table. "The kid didn't make it. The explosion killed him." There was a pause. "But from the ground, when he looked up after he fell, Allen saw movement from one of the windows a few down and hollered at one of the other firefighters. It was a woman with her dog trapped in the apartment on the floor where the fire started. She couldn't get out her door because the fire had spread into the hallway." Brian's jaw worked as he got the last sentences out. "His colleague got both of them out because Allen saw them. Even on the ground with his legs no longer working, he didn't quit doing his job."

After Sheila let Allen know in no uncertain terms that he was welcome to shove her head down onto his cock and say whatever he wanted to until he came, a beast seemed to be unleashed in the upper body of the man in front of her. He grabbed her hair, pumped her head onto his cock, pushed on her neck until his length almost gagged her. His obvious and uncontrollable urgency made Sheila's cunt wetter than it had been in a long time. She relaxed her throat, taking what he gave her, never for a second wanting it any other way.

"Yes, yes, oh god yes, suck that, slut," Allen growled, the words coming so easily that she again imagined them as a part of his regular repertoire before the bravery he embodied had culminated in this drastic change to his body, his home, his life.

Allen released his grip with one hand and rethreaded his fingers through her blonde hair. His fist twisted with an even greater furor, though not before she noticed the way he'd caressed her scalp for less than a second, a tenderness in his fingers her heart almost didn't know how to stand. Pushing her head down ever faster, he abruptly let out a suppressed groan and held her still. Sheila wasn't sure if he was ejaculating – she didn't know whether or not that could still happen – but to her it was inescapable that he was climaxing, and her own thighs trembled as she sensed rather than felt the pulsating release from his body and his being of things that had been trapped there for almost a year.

Gradually the tension in his hands faded, and he removed them from her head. Sheila rose, letting go of him slowly as she wiped her mouth delicately and helped him remove the condom. Her jaw ached, and for reasons unbeknownst to her she felt more alive than at any recent time she could remember.

When she looked up at Allen, he averted his eyes, the tears in them impossible to hide as he reached to fasten his pants. Though she would have preferred not to do so in front of him, it brought forth her own, and she stopped reaching for her skirt and sat on the floor in front of him, naked, waiting a few seconds before she reached to hold the hand that sat limply now in its position on the arm of his wheelchair.

"Allen." She had no idea what she might say, but his name came to her lips.

He looked at her. The pain in his brown eyes took her breath away, and she found herself unable to speak.

"You're going to get better." She almost blinked at the sound of her own voice; she had no idea where the statement had come from. Brian had said something about the treatment Allen was receiving, that a specialist had said there might be a way, a long time from now, for him to regain partial use of his legs. Still, her own assertion made her uncomfortable, having come from her mouth with nothing she was aware of whatsoever to back it up, but she internally shook her head and focused on the man in front of her.

He smiled, though it didn't cut the dullness that had returned to his eyes. "You're going to get better," she said again, the words again surprising her. "But know that even so, you're fine as you are right now. You're just fine." Her voice dropped to a whisper with the last sentence, and she rose to her knees, leaning to press a kiss onto the cheek that was wet against her lips. She stood and dressed silently, respecting his choice not to speak as she readied herself to walk out the door. As that moment grew closer, she felt her throat close, and she had to clear it twice before she was able to turn and bid him her final goodbye.

"It was my honor to have the chance to see you today." There was no way she could have meant it more. She leaned to kiss him, on the lips this time, and brushed her fingers over his cheek before she turned away and paced to the door. She smiled at him as she opened it, and his brown eyes rose to meet hers as she saw him struggle to smile back. She wasn't sure whether or not he intended her to hear his whispered "Thank you" as she closed the door behind her.

More

Among other things, he introduced me to Floyd that night. I know, they've been around for decades. They're classic. But somehow, all this time, I had missed them. It's possible that I will always associate the sound of Pink Floyd now with being tied up, but in any case, it struck me at some point while I was bound on my back to Max's ottoman that what I was hearing was somehow the perfect bondage music. It was as though it was made for being tied up in the dark, flickering flames of the candles around me moving more than I was able to in the position I was.

He had offered me a choice of colors. A half-dozen coils of rope sat in a neat pile in the corner of the room. Blue – both light and dark – black, green, pink. I chose purple.

Max had a fake rose in his living room. It was so perfectly and subtly formed that when I first saw it upon my arrival I didn't recognize what it was even made of. I stepped closer and saw that it was actually careful layers of feathers, placed over each other in perfect imitation of petals. Had it not been lying prone on the shelf, no vase or water in sight, I would have thought it was real.

Except that it was black.

Pink, purple, black.

Floyd, rope, rose.

Him.

Me.

The exquisiteness of this night, this session, still reduces me to one-word descriptions.

I knew about bondage, had heard stories of it, knew people who were into it. And I couldn't say I hadn't thought about it, but I had never felt the pull to try it. Truthfully, I was afraid of it. I sensed that in order to get me near a rope that I would let someone use to tie me with, there would need to be an incredible trust. A trust I wasn't sure I had ever had in anyone. Or maybe hadn't had in myself.

His hands worked efficiently, sliding just enough rope through his fingers, then around parts of my naked body, walking around me in circles as he wound it around me, through itself, over my shoulders or under my wrists. Occasionally he whipped the slack like one shakes out an extension cord before using it. The shining purple cord would jolt and dance in the air for a split second before thudding back to the floor.

I could almost feel his concentration.

He didn't look at me – at my eyes anyway. His focus was on my body. Or more so, he wasn't even focused on my body so much as the flawless rope sliding through his fingers. The only reason my body was a recipient of his attention was because it was what he was tying up with it. His eyes followed every turn of the rope and every inch of my form as he brought the two together. Every once in a while, still without looking at me, he would pause seamlessly and touch my skin, taking my breath away. The unusual feeling of the rope would be replaced by the familiar feeling of someone else's warm flesh, his hands brushing me ever so gently before he re-attended to the purple silk that never left them.

When he had me tied, he tugged gently on the ends of the rope, and I knew I was to move as he led. The ends were behind me, and I walked somewhat unsteadily backward as he walked me with assurance to the full-length mirror on the other side of the room. Once there, he turned me around to face it. And then, for the first time in almost 30 minutes, he met my gaze. In the glass.

I dropped my eyes to the systematic pattern, the purple lines now tracing over my body, my nipples peeking out of diamonds of rope. I looked at the knot directly over my clit. I had felt him forming it, of course. Now I could feel it pressing ever so slightly, waking that part of my body up for... what? What was to come?

Max turned me around by the shoulders so I could see the back of me in the mirror. Craning my neck, I studied the pattern, different but just as intricate, across my back. Max was smiling a little now, his eyes roaming over my body in the mirror. Admiring his handiwork. Or thinking of what he had in store for me.

For some reason I shuddered.

"You cold?" The first words spoken between us since

he had picked up the rope. He looked at me, eyebrows slightly raised. I shook my head quickly. He nodded once and pulled the ends of the rope again to lead me back to the center of the large room. There he carefully laid me on my back over the large ottoman. Once again he was not looking at me, but somehow every time a vague feeling of apprehension began to form inside, he would touch me. His skin to mine. After feeling only rope for several minutes at a time, that sensation took on a new significance. The connection was breathtaking.

I turned my head from my horizontal position and saw the candles lining the side of the room. The flames looked free, playful, full of movement, as though they were giggling at me as they showed off how much they could move while I lay solidly bound. I lifted my head to glance down at the shining purple coiled and knotted against my skin. Simultaneously, I heard the music. Quiet as it was, I hadn't even noticed it while he was tying me up. It was so low I couldn't even make it out.

But I could feel it. I asked what it was.

"Floyd," Max answered without looking up, working with the rope at my left thigh, coiling it around the leg of the ottoman. I strained to hear. I knew the reason I hadn't been able to identify the song was most likely because I didn't know it, but the vague musical strains captivated me. I asked the song.

"*Shine On You Crazy Diamond*," he said, rising and moving to the stereo. "Parts one through five." He turned up the volume ever so slightly, just enough that I could discern guitar strains that flowed in the background as though they were part of the air. Just as I started to listen, however, my attention was taken elsewhere.

With the final silent, firm tug Max gave the rope that secured me to the ottoman, I realized the precariousness of my position. I had known at the beginning that this was a significant undertaking for me. But the full realization didn't materialize until parts of my body, parts I was used to being able to move at will, were bound in place – and the corresponding understanding that he was now in control of that part of my existence.

I couldn't move. I was, quite literally, bound. I thought about what would happen if I suddenly couldn't breathe, if the claustrophobia of my youth returned, smothering me and taking my oxygen as I lay there unable to do anything to save myself. I thought of demanding that the rope be cut, screaming at Max to get the binding off me as quickly as possible. Would he do it? I wouldn't be asking – I would be desperate, drowning, screaming inside with not only desperation but the revulsion of knowing I was fully, completely dependent on him. That he could choose to disregard me if he wanted to. To not take me seriously.

Even as it flitted through my consciousness, the liquid hatred of the idea rose inside me and started to course through my body. My eyes were closed, but the darkness I was seeing was more than physical – I believe I would have seen it just as much had they been open, staring at the candlelit white ceiling of Max's living room.

Max touched me. My eyes flew open. He wasn't looking at me. Rather, he was examining the twists of rope at my left hip, his fingers resting softly on my left thigh. The contact had brought me from darkness to the surface like a flash of lightning. I inhaled deeply.

"That's better," he murmured in a tone as soft as the

pressure of his fingers on my thigh. "You okay now?" Still he did not look at me. His attention stayed on the purple silk strands around my hips and up across my abdomen, as though there were some imperfection there he was fixing. And I wondered how he had known. I was fairly certain I had made no noise.

When I didn't answer, he finally turned to me. His brown eyes were infinite; in them I saw the darkness where I had just been and the light that was transferring to me now through his touch. I couldn't speak.

I heard the music again. There was singing now. As unfamiliar with them as I'd been upon entering the room an hour before, I could tell it was Pink Floyd.

"What song is this one?" My voice returned for the sake of the curiosity stirring in me.

"Same song."

The volume was such that I could just barely make out the words, and I was surprised by his answer. Could it really have been so few minutes since I first asked what was playing?

"It's a long song," he continued. "Two songs, actually. This is the first one."

Before I could ask more questions, Max leaned over me and traced his fingers down my right side, making me tense and try to squirm away from him as the sensation tickled my skin. He increased the pressure until it no longer tickled but made me squirm differently, my body suddenly wanting something I noticed with a shock I hadn't even been thinking about. I blinked in surprise.

Max shifted his hand. I felt the knot I had noticed earlier move slightly against my clit. The jolt of arousal that flooded through me stunned me as much with its intensity as with its unexpectedness. I looked at Max, who met my gaze and knew what he saw there.

He smiled. "It's not about fucking tonight, Amber. Don't you know that by now? You think that's what you want, but what you want is so much more." His voice was quiet, a contrast to the newfound desire pulsing through me that didn't feel quiet. Confusion gripped me, twisting my inside with a movement my physical body wasn't at liberty to reflect.

Max stood and walked until he was no longer in my field of vision. I heard him kneel behind the top of my head, and his warmth reached me before he did as he slid one hand through my hair and the other gently around my throat from behind. His lips touched my ear as he whispered into it. The sensation shot through me like a gunshot, starkly contrasting with the barely existent contact of his flesh with mine. What was he doing to me?

"Let go. Let go, Amber. Do you hear me?" His voice ran like liquid silk, its gentle seamlessness giving no hint of the boulder-like intimidation of the order as my mind perceived it. The voice was gentle, lulling, leading me where it wanted to take me, knowing that was a place I wasn't sure I had ever been. So much so that I didn't know where it was or how to find it. The fierce resistance inside me reappeared, searing my senses as it surged furiously. A snowy fuzziness filled my vision. An acidic sour seeped into my mouth as I raged against this position he had me in.

And somewhere even deeper, I saw that I was really in a battle against myself.

The voice knew that too. The grip on my throat tightened ever so slightly. The heat of his breath coursed through me via my ear:

"I know you don't know how, Amber. That's what I'm here for."

Never since that night has the song not transported me back there. In the six months since, I've listened to every single Pink Floyd song I could find. When I listened to *Shine On You Crazy Diamond*, which of course came first, I found it was some of the most beautiful guitar playing I'd ever heard. The spectrum of Floyd, from the searching lyrics of Syd Barrett to the spellbinding guitar of David Gilmour to the hypnotizing voice of Roger Waters and everything in between, has pulled out of me things I never knew were there, things that seem still to spill forth from a darkness in me that was ripped open with an intensity I can barely remember as I lay bound on my back listening to *Shine On You Crazy Diamond, Pts. 1-5*, for the very first time.

Standing now a few feet from Steven in his bedroom, I have been transported. Steven doesn't know about my night with Max. It happened before I met him. And right now he likely thinks nothing of the song that has begun to emerge from the stereo speakers behind him. Although he is watching me, I know he doesn't know I am no longer there, standing in front of him as I was seconds ago.

Though the volume on his stereo is low, the unmistakable synthesizer cuts through the dim background in my head like the only colored object in a black-and-white photograph. It is mere seconds into the song, and my vision is now of candlelight, a black rose made of feathers lying motionless on the shelf, purple silk and pale flesh. I cannot move.

"Amber?" Steven says my name. He takes a step closer to me. I feel myself breathe.

It comes. Sudden release slams through me like the breath of the universe, electrifying every atom that I am. My eyes snap back into focus, connecting with Steven's clear blue ones as I move into him without a word. Our mouths become one, a writhing, pulsing dance of connection both receiving and feeding the lasers of raw heat shooting through my body. I push against him so hard he falls to the bed behind him, and I attack him like a volcano erupting, like the heat radiating from my body is melting us, welding us together. Restraint is nonexistent.

Which had never happened to me before my night with Max.

Steven grabs my hair, shoving his hips against me. I can feel the stiffness of his cock through his jeans. I reach down to rip them open, the ferocity of unbridled lust firing through me. He yanks his jeans the rest of the way off and I jump back on him, nearly smothering him in my desire to fuck him now. He slips on a condom amidst my mauling and pushes up into me. My gasp is almost a scream, but I have been quiet and remain so, the only sound I hear my frantic breathing as I buck against him in a ravenous explosion. The energy in me feels somehow too deep inside to come all the way to the surface as sound.

I am focused on Steven, I know. But my experience with Max, that one and only night I was with him, is an inextricable part of what is happening now. Because it is a part of me.

Steven drives up into me, hard, his grunting louder than my breathing, and I am riding, riding him like a force of its own, one I'm not even controlling. My orgasm starts, and I'm not sure if he is even touching me. His hard cock fills me, but I don't know if his fingers are on my clit or not. The wave crashes through me and I fall against him, still coming, still flying, not aware if I'm making noise, letting go of everything that is in me, that is me, so that for this moment, I don't know where or even who I am.

It recedes. I am lying flat on top of Steven, breathing heavily. He is still fucking me, holding me by the hips and ramming into me, squeezing me harder and harder as he gets closer, as I can tell from his breathing. When he lets go I bring my arms against his body, holding him as close as I can while he comes inside me, his moan in my ear, my cheek pressed against his neck.

The song is still playing. *Shine On You Crazy Diamond, Pts. 1-5.* I can hear Roger Waters singing now, and I know the song is near the end of its thirteen and a half minutes. I lie motionless, my breath hard to catch.

The truth is, I don't really know what Max did to me that night. One of the things I learned from him was how much I don't know.

The saxophone starts, and I am on my back, purple rope holding me in place as I gaze up at a candlelit white ceiling feeling something move in me I still don't know how to describe. Steven runs a hand gently through my hair. I move my hand to rest in his as I close my eyes, candlelight flickering behind them as the notes fade around us.

Safe

Ericka's breath billowed around her as she rang the doorbell and waited for Maureen or Jeremy – or any of their assorted guests – to answer. A car whizzed by on the street behind her, and she jumped, glancing over her shoulder at the now-empty asphalt below the gray winter sky.

The door opened, and Ericka whirled back around. Maureen invited her in with a flourish, and Ericka willed her adrenaline to subside as she stepped into the room.

A small roar erupted from the dozen people all dressed in the same colors gathered in front of the TV. "Touchdown," Maureen explained with a smile. She touched Ericka's shoulder briefly as she closed the door, a calming gesture only a friend as attuned and thoughtful as Maureen would know to do. Ericka smiled back as she set the fruit salad she carried on the food table and slipped out of her coat.

Something else happened that pleased the small

crowd in the room, and Ericka turned to the television. She didn't follow football, but she was happy for the many of their friends who did that sat in the living room now watching the hometown team playing in the Super Bowl. She located the numbers at the bottom of the screen. The score was in their favor.

Ericka's eyes went to the people gathered in the room, and her heartbeat picked up as she spotted Sam, his eyes beamed like a laser toward the flat screen on the wall. She smiled to herself. She knew he was a big fan of football and an even bigger fan of the team he was watching now play the biggest game of the season. In the three years she'd been acquainted with him, she'd seen him and Jeremy and numerous other of their friends doggedly cheering on a team that had fallen short time and time again when it came to the playoffs. She'd known Sam would be excited about this. Obviously she was right.

He was also, truthfully, one of the reasons she'd shown up at this party today, and she was even gladder to have been right about the likelihood of his being there.

She wasn't sure what accounted for the magnetic attraction she'd experienced toward Sam from the second she'd met him at a similar party three years before. She'd been with Neal then, so she hadn't had – or hadn't taken – the chance to find out if what she felt for Sam was returned. The next gathering at which she'd seen him, he'd had a date with him. And so it had gone, with one or the other of them with somebody throughout the three years she had known him. They'd always caught up, though, sneaking – at least it had always felt that way to her – away from their respective partners long enough to exchange something that had always seemed to her, though not overtly, more than pleasantries.

During a time-out now, Sam glanced her way. He did a double take when he saw her.

"Ericka!" He stood and leaned over the back of the couch, and she moved forward to receive his friendly hug. Taking a surreptitious inventory of the people sitting near him, she saw no one unfamiliar and deduced he was there alone. A spark jumped from her stomach to her pussy.

Jeremy yelled something at the TV, and Sam turned quickly, adding his own retort to the man in black-and-white stripes on the screen before turning back to her. As he held her gaze, Ericka found herself thinking not for the first time that either her interest in him was mutual, or he had an uncanny flirtatiousness that could make anyone he looked at like that think it was. Smiling coyly, she averted her eyes.

"Come sit," he said, turning back around and scooting over to make room for her on the couch. Ericka caught her breath. The opportunity wasn't one she was about to pass up, and she moved to the front of the couch and waited for another whistle before greeting everyone and crossing in front of several people to squeeze in beside him. Her pussy contracted almost painfully at the invited closeness.

Sam took a swig of his beer. "Oh, come on," he protested, his words almost lost in the general assent that went up as a referee made another call against their team. The next moment he'd jumped forward in his seat, his strong form close to the edge of the couch as someone in the same kind of jersey he wore took off with the football across the field.

Ericka smiled even as she winced a bit at the volume of the triumphant shout that filled the room. When Sam sat back, he gave her a smile that sparkled like a Fourth-of-July finale, and his enthusiasm made her want him more than ever.

Of course, she'd always wanted Sam. Ever since she'd met him, which included the last month and a half of her and Neal's relationship, she had thought about him frequently. There was no question that she was interested in fucking him. But she liked him beyond that too – which was rather an anomaly for her.

Ericka felt the urge to fidget nervously and took a deep breath. Her usual MO was to sleep with people for a brief time – usually, if she were to admit it, until the emotional part started to get more serious than the sexual part – and then move on. The juxtaposition of having become acquainted with Sam enough to feel like they were close to friends while having been attracted to him the whole time (but not fucking him) was new to her. She tried to remember the last time she'd been interested in someone for such a long time without acting on it. She couldn't.

What was even stranger to her was that a lot of people seemed to find that mode of operating perfectly natural. It was something she didn't understand. Sex with someone she felt close to had always felt scary to her, and thus quite unappealing. Truth be told, she preferred to fuck people she didn't know.

She jumped as the spectators around her whooped, and she turned her attention to what was happening on the screen. Of course, that wasn't very helpful since she didn't understand what was happening on the screen, but it seemed to please the audience in Maureen and

Jeremy's living room. As Ericka reached for a cracker from the tray on the coffee table, Sam's hand brushed her shoulder as he moved it to rest along the back of the couch behind her. Her breath caught, her stomach immediately rearranging itself to no longer invite food.

Moments later the crowd broke up to refill drinks and ambush the food table as halftime began. Sam turned to her.

"So, how've you been?"

She smiled and dropped her eyes, besieged by a sudden shyness at his sincere attention. She mustered an answer but quickly moved to deflect the attention back to him. "How about you?"

"I'm doing well. I've started to look for a house. My roommate moved out about a month ago, and I can't really afford the rent on my own. Might be time to think about buying."

"Oh, you live by yourself now?" For some reason the idea made Ericka's stomach turn a slow somersault. She realized some vague part of her consciousness had always assumed they would never have a physical location to be alone even if they'd had the opportunity, as they had always seen each other at gatherings, and each of them had roommates. The thrill from Sam's revelation surprised her, and Ericka bit her lip, the cracker a forgotten relic between her fingers.

When the game resumed, Ericka was having trouble sitting still between the physical proximity to Sam and the awareness that he would go home to an empty apartment after he left there. The excitement of the game, even though she had no idea what was going on in it, kept her adrenaline on high, which, coupled with her immediate attraction, translated directly into arousal. With two minutes left on the play clock, she could feel the tension in Sam as he zeroed in on the TV. The heat emanating from his body made her want to jump on him. She tried to focus instead on the whistles and commentary and announcements coming from the surround-sound speakers.

After lots of stops and starts of the game clock that she didn't understand, play resumed, and some of the people in the room rose to their feet as the seconds ticked down. Ericka wasn't sure what was happening, but she had the impression it was favorable as the suspense in the room heightened. Abruptly the friends around her exploded into pandemonium, screaming and jumping and hugging as similar antics occurred on the screen among the coaches and players dressed in the same colors as most of the occupants of the room.

Ericka deduced their team had just won the Super Bowl.

Sam turned and pulled her to her feet, and she laughed as he swept her into a hug. As he set her down, his lips pressed against hers in a moment of giddy exuberance, and she caught her breath as he pulled away almost as quickly to continue celebrating. Her body tingled as she watched the glee around her, a newfound exhilaration of her own pulsing from her core.

Soon Sam turned back to her. "I'm sorry – I hope that was okay," he said near her ear. His smile was a bit sheepish as he backed up to look her in the eye. "My excitement got the better of me for a second."

Ericka met his eyes squarely. "Lucky for me."

Sam's expression shifted, and the noise around them

seemed to dull as he looked at her for an extended moment. He appeared to hesitate, as though working to find words, and Ericka was just about to relieve him of the effort when he spoke.

"Would you like to come home with me?"

Ericka couldn't hold back a breathless chuckle. She stepped closer to him, holding his gaze. "Are you happy your team just won?"

Sam's grin was electrifying, and he took her hand as they turned to find their coats.

Ericka had never been in Sam's apartment before, and her core buzzed with excitement at the prospect as he unlocked the door.

"It's a little sparse right now," he said as he led her inside, closing the door behind her. "Cody took his furniture with him, of course."

Indeed the only things in the open, square room were the understated entertainment center in a corner below a flat screen-TV, the L-shaped burgundy couch opposite it, and a mahogany coffee table in between.

Ericka, however, felt little concern about the furniture or any lack of it.

"Do you want a tour, or do you want – ?" Sam began, and Ericka turned to him. He broke off his own sentence as she stepped toward him, and his mouth landed on hers with an urgency this time, stealing her breath as her body plunged immediately into craving mode.

Sam swept her from her feet and carried her to the couch, and she reached for his belt buckle as he set her on the burgundy leather. Reaching to help her, he ripped his pants open and pulled off his shirt before reaching for hers. Breathlessly she sat up, helping him pull her sweater off before she lay back and he unzipped her jeans. Sam held up a finger and disappeared for a second. Ericka smiled as he reappeared and dropped a strip of condoms on the coffee table.

Then he lowered himself on top of her, and the weight of his body made her sigh as she wrapped her legs around him and he kissed her again. After a moment, Sam slid off of her and reached between her legs.

She sucked in her breath as his fingertip brushed her clit. Slowly, almost lazily, his finger found a feathering rhythm. Despite the unhurried nature of his movements, Ericka knew he was watching her acutely, paying attention to the signals her body was giving in response to his contact. That was the kind of man he was. As the thought occurred to her, she realized she had somehow known that since the moment she'd met him.

She recognized the sensation that threatened to take her over the brink. As the impending climax drew closer, she bit her lip and performed her usual tactic.

"Fuck me," she whispered, squirming subtly away from his touch and spreading her legs.

Sam grinned, slipping his hand back to where it had been on her flesh. "Oh, I will," he agreed as he held her gaze. "Right after I make you come."

Ericka swallowed. She'd suspected Sam would be more difficult than most men. She wondered briefly if she could simply relax and let it happen, but the moment the thought flickered through her consciousness, anxiety rose physically in her body. She squelched both the idea and the sensation and pushed Sam back, rolling on top of him.

"But I want you now," she whispered, her pussy growing even wetter at the idea of his being inside of her.

Sam's smile was indulgent. "That's mutual – but you couldn't possibly mind if I get you off first, could you?"

His tone was playful, light. If only he knew.

Ericka opened her mouth to say something but stopped, not knowing what it should be. She felt her cheeks flush and knew he noticed because he raised his eyebrows. Caught now in the inevitable awkwardness when this wasn't handled correctly, Ericka ducked her head. Before he could ask a question, she spoke.

"I actually prefer not to have other people make me come." She shrugged, her voice sounding casual even to her ears. To her, it was a casual revelation, though it had never failed to surprise everyone she'd told. Still, in most cases it hadn't been an issue – once she said she'd rather just be fucked, most men had acquiesced.

Sam smiled a bit incredulously. "Why on earth would you not want to come?"

"I didn't say I didn't want to come. I just don't like for other people to do it for me." Ericka smiled, trying to keep her tone light. "I can make myself come just fine. Getting fucked is what I prefer. I can't do that to myself – I can't hold myself down and fuck myself hard like I like it." Just saying the words made her breathing change, and she willed him to jump on her and do just that.

Her narration appeared to have a similar effect on Sam, who shifted a bit as his cock twitched. "Well, I would certainly love to do that for you." His voice was low, and she felt the moisture increase between her thighs at the look in his eyes. "Do you mean though that you'd like to get yourself off first?"

Ericka shrugged. Whether or not she had an orgasm was not her main concern regarding sex. She'd meant what she said – an orgasm was something she could give herself. Being taken the way the way something deep inside her almost constantly seemed to want was something she could only get from someone else.

Sam looked perplexed at her hesitation, and she tried to ward off the impatience she felt. She just wanted him inside her. She said as much, and Sam gave a soft groan as he reached to grip his cock lightly.

"Show me," he said, nodding to her as he slid his hand slowly up his shaft. "Show me how you come first. Then I'll hold you down and fuck you till you can't see straight."

With that promise on the table, Ericka needed no further convincing. She fell back against the leather and reached between her legs, not surprised to feel the moisture dripping there. Her finger landed on her clit, and she pressed firmly.

It was striking how different her own method of making herself come was from what it took for someone else to bring her to orgasm. When she got herself off, it was rough, fast, no-nonsense – much like how she liked to be fucked. Solid pressure, firm rhythm, single-minded aim. With Sam watching, she began this ritual now, holding his gaze as she gasped and arched her back at the helm of her own fingers.

For a man to make her come, he could only barely touch her. Careful. Gentle. Delicate even.

Rarely did she allow it.

The truth was, orgasm at the hands – or whatever part

– of another person put that person in control, took her out of it, placed her in a position of vulnerability with which she was uncomfortable, no matter how physically pleasurable it might be. Taking a hard, pounding cock, making positively a puddle between her legs as it slammed into her – that wasn't challenging. On the contrary, she loved it. Going slowly, feeling, being handled kindly, gently – that felt difficult. Almost intolerable, actually.

The trauma therapist to whom Ericka had been referred had talked with her about dissociation, about being dissociated from her body. More specifically, she'd brought up the idea of possible strategies Ericka's psyche employed to allow her to be in her body. Things like unconsciously relinquishing control and then yearning for someone outside her to force her into it in a way that felt safe to her – by, for example, fucking her. But it had to be fast, rough, no time for the death-fear to creep in that happened when she was actually consciously led to focus on her body.

Shoving the contemplation from her mind, Ericka focused on Sam. As she did, a sudden shyness emerged, and she looked away from him. He was watching her avidly, his hand on his cock, but not in a self-centered way – more as a necessity, like he was communicating with it to hold on, acknowledging what it wanted and telling it to wait while he got something he wanted too.

Ericka flushed again, a wave of unease fluttering over her. She liked Sam. It was ironic that that made this harder.

But it wasn't unfamiliar.

Sam met her eyes when she paused, and she looked away. Her desire for him to fuck her now was almost desperate.

"Sam," she said, injecting every bit of the true lust she felt into the word and hoping it would cover the desperation she knew was just beneath its surface. "Please fuck me."

"Come," he said. His voice was almost pleading. "Please, Ericka."

She held his gaze for a moment. God, he cared. He seriously cared. He cared if she came, and he cared about her. The urge to throw herself into his arms suddenly battled with the urge to ride his cock, and she shuddered. They were not congruent.

Unnerved, she nodded, resuming her position. She had barely returned her fingers to her clit when she was coming, crying out and reaching for him with her other hand. Sam jolted to his knees, grabbing a condom from the coffee table and almost ripping it in half in his haste to get it unwrapped.

When he sank into her, she was surprised to feel herself almost burst into tears. She held her breath, willing the reaction to subside even as a combination of sublimeness and connection made her feel almost dizzy. She wrapped her arms around Sam, clinging tight to his shoulders as he slammed into her with what she suddenly knew was the same connection she was experiencing.

Her body began to shake. Tears emerged that she knew had nothing to do with him, and she fought to push them back.

He pulled away slightly. "Are you okay?"

Ericka nodded, quickly, the awareness that he wasn't going to understand increasing the near panic she had ironically wanted him to eviscerate. Sam started to pull out.

"No!" The word broke through a tightness in her body she desperately wanted to be rid of. Feeling his cock in her, hard, fast, unrelenting, was the only way she knew how to get that to happen. She clung to him as she wondered frantically how to convey what she needed, to make him understand she wasn't upset with him or by anything he was doing. "Please don't stop." Her voice was tiny, mournful.

Like a child's.

Sam pulled away, and the void was excruciating. Her breath stopped as her body screamed for the pressure of his to return.

"Ericka, what's wrong?"

She couldn't speak or even move enough to swipe at the tear that fell as she closed her eyes. She felt Sam get up from the couch and recognized the swirl of panic that erupted in her core, seeping into her cells and enveloping just enough of them to take over her consciousness, keep her from breaking free of the physical trauma cycle they'd talked about in her sessions.

"No," she said again, the sob breaking forth.

"Ericka, I'm really sorry. I don't know what I did to upset you, but whatever it was, I absolutely didn't mean to."

"Sam," she moaned, the energy to explain sweeping from her like a dried leaf in the wind. Her head dropped to the cushion, her body trembling as Sam looked at her.

"It's not you. It's not you, Sam. I know that doesn't make sense." She was fighting to breathe by this time, and Sam was looking more and more alarmed as he watched her. Ericka flushed with humiliation, knowing he was upset and that no explanation she gave was going to make sense or perhaps even relieve him of feeling like he'd done something wrong.

"Ericka, I promise I didn't mean to do anything you didn't want me to."

She shook her head frantically, not knowing how to make him understand. "That didn't happen. I want you. I've always wanted you, and I want you now. You – you make me feel safe." The words frightened her even as they slipped out, and she closed her eyes against the tears that blurred his form in front of her. "I just want to feel safe."

Her voice had retreated to a whisper. Sam appeared unconvinced, and something inside her deflated. It wasn't working. He didn't understand, and at that moment she knew she had probably scared him off from ever touching her again. As if to confirm her silent recognition of defeat, Sam gently picked up her clothes and set them near her on the coffee table, then walked silently from the room.

Ericka sobbed quietly on the couch, the shame flooding her face making it feel hot as an iron. She didn't know how long she lay there alone in Sam's living room, humiliation saturating her body, before she managed to pull herself up. Almost dizzily, she wrapped herself in the blanket tossed over the back of the couch and went to the kitchen. Her limbs felt numb as she located a glass and filled it from the tap.

Standing at the sink, Ericka stared at the plain white wall in front of her, a nondescript wooden cabinet a foot above where the stainless steel met the paint. Her breath felt hard to catch, and it wasn't for the reason she'd hoped when she'd shown up here. She felt a sob forming and used all her energy to will her breath into evenness.

She was to let herself out, she knew. Sam was in another room, and she knew he wasn't planning to say goodbye. The idea of walking out the door brought a new wave of dread. She didn't count on seeing him again; she wasn't sure he would even talk to her anymore.

She'd undergone enough therapy to know that just as what her body was reacting to wasn't about him, what she really wanted wasn't about him either – and she would be okay without him. But intellectual awareness wasn't the same as true embodiment, and the panic she felt now was one that had had the historic power to overtake her awareness again and again.

Tears pushed their way forward as she set the glass on the counter, preparing to back away from the sink. Instead her body froze, and she set her hands on the silver coolness and squeezed her eyes shut for a few seconds as she waited for it to stop shaking. It hadn't ceased doing so since she and Sam had been on the couch.

She heard a noise and turned just in time to see Sam cross the kitchen in three strides. Shock made her breath stop in her throat as he caught her and wrapped his arms around her from behind, holding hers against her body like a vise. His mouth was near her ear.

"You're safe with me, baby." His whispered voice was rough, urgent. His solid form pressed against her back as his embrace held her arms, her whole body, in place between himself and the counter. "Do you hear me? You're safe with me."

The words brought forth a rush of fluid between her legs, and her strength left her as she sagged against his grasp. It tightened, not letting her fall, and she made an incoherent sound as she felt him pause a split second before removing one hand and sliding it slowly down her hip.

"Do you want me to fuck you?" His grip had turned to iron, his voice like redemption in her ear.

Her "*yes*" was strangled, pushing forth faster than her system had the capacity to articulate.

Sam pulled her hips back and pushed her legs apart with his knees. Ericka had her wits about her enough to hiss "Condom" over her shoulder as she tensed away from him for a second.

"I have one on."

Surprised, Ericka craned her neck and looked down. Sam took a half step back to show her, and she raised startled eyes to his.

"I told you, you're safe with me." He held her gaze for a moment before he stepped back into her, crushing his lips against hers as he held the back of her head. She knew when he wrenched away and positioned her body against the counter that it was because he couldn't stand to not be inside her for another second, and it took her breath away.

Sam pushed into her, holding her solidly as he fucked her hard and kissed the back of her neck gently, the stark juxtaposition scrambling the signals inside her that didn't know what to do. Except fuck. She took his cock, allowing herself to be shoved into her body as though from the outside, the only way she'd ever found to be in it that didn't feel like it would destroy her – that, on the contrary, sometimes felt so incredible that she felt like she could actually be with it, be with what was in her, with all of herself, and feel like the world was okay.

Suddenly Sam's fingertip was against her clitoris.

Ericka gasped and tried to struggle away, but he held her tight.

"You're safe, Ericka. Do you hear me? I'm right here. I've got you. You're safe." The whisper started a raging fire within her, and she squirmed as it began to gather and sear toward the place where his gentle fingers met her flesh. Sam's grip was unmovable, and suddenly she screamed over and over as the surrender ripped through her, as she came with his name on her lips and his cock in her cunt and his finger on her clit sobbing and scared and euphoric and knowing he was fully in control and aware of exactly what he was doing. All strength, as well as all tension – and for a moment she wondered if something in her saw them as the same thing – evaporated as she collapsed against the cold counter in front of her. Sam's grip on her tightened, invincible, unmovable, there to hold what inside of her she had somehow never managed to hold herself.

Ericka felt barely conscious. She sensed Sam coming, and even then, he held on to her, his climax seeming like a calm, beautiful, far-away release compared to what she had just undergone. When he pulled out, he kept holding her as she let her head fall forward, and even as she began crying quietly, he didn't let go. *He didn't let go.*

Ericka knocked on the door, hoping none of the neighbors appeared while she waited for Sam to answer. However cathartic they'd felt to her, she doubted any of the people who shared walls with him had appreciated her vocal acrobatics last time she'd been there.

The door opened. "Hey, Ericka." Sam's smile looked exactly as it had earlier in the week when he'd first caught sight of at her at the Super Bowl party. It made her breath catch a little, and she paused for a second before stepping inside. What happened now? Where did they go from here? She barely remembered what had taken place after Sam had left her in the living room the last time she was here.

Her mind barely remembered, anyway. Her body seemed to know as she felt it energetically reaching for him, propelling her toward him like a magnet.

Without a word Sam stepped forward and put his arms around her. Her body tensed, afraid of the gesture, of the very kindness it embodied. Sam didn't withdraw. Ericka took a deep breath and felt the childlike neediness rise inside of her as she pressed against him. His stance stayed the same as she kept breathing, frowning at the turmoil she could sense developing under the surface of her skin.

In an instant, the clinginess passed. She marveled that what her therapist had said seemed true – that if she stayed with things, observed rather than ran from them, they often moved right through just like clouds passing over the moon.

Ericka focused on the warmth in her body. Her body, which was coming to grips with her sudden awareness of it, her – however slight – capacity to be in it, to pay attention to it as she walked through the store, put the car in drive, lay down to go to bed, bit into an apple.

It was foreign to her. Still, the very fact that she knew that felt monumental.

Feeling her physical form now beyond the dissociated projections she usually identified with brought a wave of terror, and she shook. Sam still didn't move, neither tightening nor loosening his grip as her body moved involuntarily, his embrace solid like the protection she'd never known, never learned to find and engage in herself. The familiar physical craving reared up, stronger this time, and she breathed with it too, waiting for it to pass.

When the desperation subsided, Ericka knew her cunt was getting wet for reasons other than an unconscious illusion. She pulled away enough for her mouth to meet Sam's, and he pressed into her with a kiss she did her best to feel beyond the explosion it elicited in her pussy, to connect at the same time with the man that stood behind it, holding her with all the capacity to love and rage and fuck and lust and heal and err and cherish a human being had. All the things that were in her too.

She raised one leg and pushed her thigh against his hip as Sam kissed her harder, backing her up against the wall as he grasped the back of her knee and ground himself into her. Ericka's breath caught as the jolt from her clit shot up through her core, spilling from her throat in a low moan.

Sam couldn't be her savior. She knew that. Nobody could. The safety, the protection she needed, that something in her craved so deeply, were inside her – and only her. She could never truly get them from anyone else. Ericka felt herself tremble as Sam's gentle fingers brushed the bare skin of her arm. She had a long way to go.

But she had to start somewhere.

CPSIA information can be obtained at www.ICGtesting.com
Printed in the USA
BVOW08s0203080915

417002BV00001B/5/P